THE
COLOURS
OF
DENIAL

ARTI MANANI

ISBN: 978 1 6596 1293 6

For my niece, Shreya

Keep shining

ABOUT THE AUTHOR

Arti Manani is a passionate writer and marketer, born in West London, England. She fell in love with books in her early childhood and wrote her first short story when she was ten, on scrap paper bound together by treasury tags.

The Colours of Denial is her first novel.

Find Arti on Instagram @Author_Arti_Manani
#TheColoursOfDenial

CHAPTER **ONE**

The man with the blurred face is getting closer. She's increased her pace but beneath her feet, the sharp grains of sand blackened by the darkness pulls her down into the ground, working her harder to leave the shadows. The clouds have encroached across the moon and the desert is dim, leaving her with no company other than the figures created inside her head. Her heart is pumping against her chest, with each beat louder than the one before and each breath heavier, as she comes to realise that she may not get away. Away from the darkness, the shadows and this unknown man with the blurred face. Her legs are weak and heavy and she begins to slow down until eventually she stops running, accepting her defeat. The sun will soon rise, threatening to expose her. She has nowhere to hide.

The sound of breathlessness fades as her heart

slows. Light appears in the distance as the sun gently pushes its way through the blackness. She stands, as she witnesses this miraculous fight between light and dark. The sun, so powerful that not even the shadows can defeat it, begins to celebrate its victory by showing off its vibrant, fiery colours across the skies, sprinkling the desert with gold dust. Even the clouds have surrendered and in this moment, she is calm. The world is still and silent. She stands motionless, feeling content. She is embraced by the sun's heat. Safe. Warm. The man with the blurred face has disappeared.

***

Sunday, 17 September 2017, 4:45 a.m. The curtains were drawn but the dim light from the street lamp outside her window came flooding in, casting dark, creepy figures across the room. Sophia lay in bed, tucked beneath her thick duvet staring at the ceiling, recalling her latest nightmare. The man was getting closer. A drop of sweat trickled from Sophia's forehead and down the side of her face. It was only a matter of time until she would fall asleep, and it was only a matter of time until she would be face to face with this mysterious man who had been watching her, following her, haunting her in her dreams.

She turned her body and glanced over at Oliver as he slept beside her. His long, curly, brown hair swept across his face as he lay there, peacefully. She wanted to wake him from his sleep, to talk to him, to tell him about her nightmare. She wanted him to comfort her and tell her she was safe. But he was asleep, snoring gently beside her, calm and still. A deep sigh of disappointment escaped from her mouth as she disregarded the thought of waking him, slowly turning to move into her original position. She lay on her back once again, lost in her duvet, wide awake as she stared at the blank ceiling.

Cold sweat continued to seep from her pores as her mind became hazy, clouded by the happenings of her recent nightmares. She was unable to forget, no matter how hard she tried. A secured box that was buried deep inside her was forcing itself open, compelling her to recall some of her previous encounters with the man with the blurred face. The danger wasn't real, but she was terrified. She lay there, trying to stay afloat in a pool of memories that were weighing her down, and drowning her in her own thoughts. It didn't matter that Oliver had been sleeping beside her. Sophia felt alone as she suffocated in the silence that surrounded her. It was the same silence which would later be interrupted by all of the nasty voices inside her head, as they constantly reminded her that she was not alone.

Sophia's eyes were heavy and tired but she refused to give her body what it was asking for. She refused to let herself fall asleep or rest, in fear of being tormented by another nightmare. The man with the blurred face had been getting too close, too fast.

She wasn't ready. She clenched on to her duvet as she pulled it up, tucking it under her chin, covering her body as if the duvet was a shield against her fears. She moved her arms beneath the covers, resting them by her sides as she lay there still, quiet and afraid as her armour failed to do the job she intended it to.

The voices inside her head had awakened from their peace as they hissed in whisper through her ears. They slithered inside Sophia's mind and through her thoughts, entrancing her under a spell of anxiety, spilling all of her worries that she had stored away. Her dark thoughts spilled like a large coffee overflowing in an espresso cup. The coffee was bitter and strong, full of caffeine. It was a drug she didn't like, an addiction of darkness that was embedded inside her. It was a coffee being served without a smile, and one that she didn't want to drink.

The voices inside her head would strike her often, forcing open a box of instincts, gut feelings, and signs that she had ignored and buried within. Yet no matter how far down it was hidden, the truth remained on the surface of her soul and the voices would be sure to remind her.

The voices continued to hiss at her as the drums of her heartbeat throbbed through her ears. She began to fight the snakes inside her, pushing the lid back onto the box, forcing it down. She lay there, breathing deeply while releasing some of her nicer thoughts as they soaked up the bitterness of the spilt coffee like a sponge. She lay there, trying to recreate the safe zone that had once existed.

Her bed was a place of security, where she could escape and lock herself away and be free. It was her hiding place. A place to run away where no-one would disturb her. It was the place where she could be herself, weak and sensitive, without the need to pretend that she was anything else. But the safe zone was no more, the voices inside her head told her so. Safety had become a distant memory and her safe zone was transformed into a place surrounded by dark and evil thoughts. It had become a place where she'd have many sleepless nights where she'd force herself to stay awake with no choice but to listen to the torturous voices inside her head. It had become a place where she would eventually fall asleep and be tormented in her nightmares. Her bed had become a place where she could no longer run or hide.

She turned around, grabbing on to what was left of her consciousness as she slipped out from beneath the duvet, snuggling her feet into her navy blue slipper boots. It was cold on the other side of the duvet, cold and gloomy. But she was better off.

Sophia tiptoed over to the silhouette of her overly busy dressing table, quietly, trying not to wake up Oliver. She picked up her hairbrush from its assigned area, nudging a jewellery box out of the way at the same time. Bad move. The box pushed a bottle of Chanel perfume off the table and she jolted her left arm forward to save it from smashing against the wooden interior of their bedroom floor. Saved. But a slight touch of her elbow to a can of hair spray sent it tumbling to the floor. It was dark after-all and inevitable given the state of her dressing table. The hair spray was not hers and had no assigned place on this dressing table. If Oliver were to wake up now, it was his own doing. But he didn't flinch, oblivious to his surroundings.

Sophia began to comb her hair - fine and golden like the desert sands that haunted her in her sleep, each strand glowing like the rays of sun that had been threatening to expose her to the dark shadows, and to the man with the blurred face. The hair spray rolled towards Oliver's abandoned exercise bike near the window, which now served a purpose of being a dumping ground for clothes. She glanced over at him. Despite the noise, he didn't move. He lay still, fast asleep, peacefully.

'Sorry,' she apologised in a whisper. 'About to head out for a jog.' Sophia put the hairbrush back in its allocated spot, ignoring the hair spray on the floor. She grabbed her running clothes that had been hanging from the handle bars of the exercise bike, before leaving the room.

She switched on the light as she entered the bathroom and stood at the basin, squinting and blinking as her eyes readjusted to the brightness of the large, round, moon-like ceiling light. She stared at her reflection in a small, oval mirror which sat on a little shelf above the sink. The mirror had a blue and green mosaic tile border around it. Some of the tiles were missing and the mirror itself had a chip not too far off from the centre. Despite its current state, she held on to it.

Sophia smiled at her reflection, staring at herself beyond the cracks and chips. She looked strong and controlled, independent, powerful, feisty, confident. She looked like everything she was not. She stood out, like a lion in a field of green, living in an environment that wasn't made for her, where she was always seen, but made to hide. The shades of golds and browns in her hair, the shape and depth of her large, orangey brown eyes, and her buttoned nose were very much like the features of a lion. She played a perfectly good role in holding up the appearance of being strong and courageous, but she hid the real animal inside her, always afraid, always looking out for danger, always running away - Sophia, the meerkat.

She turned on the tap and began to wash away the sweat from her face as the ice cold water began to steal her warmth. She changed into her black leggings and Oliver's baggy sweatshirt and stood there, soothed by the scent of his Armani aftershave as she closed her eyes and held her breath. The scent filled her with gratitude and awe as she reconnected with herself, embracing the steadiness of her soul with Oliver's. She exhaled slowly as she looked into the mirror proudly before turning to exit the bathroom.

Sophia headed down the stairs, quietly, slipping her feet out of her navy blue slipper boots, and into her black and orange trainers, stuffing bits of her mane into a bun at the same time.

The front door instantly slammed shut behind her. She jumped as the sound echoed through her ears, spilling more coffee from the overflowing cup inside her head. Flashbacks of the nightmare from nearly seven months ago came back to haunt her, when the man with a blurred face first came knocking on her door.

'No,' Sophia whispered to herself as she turned away from the house. She jogged down the steps and onto the street, telling herself that she was not going to be afraid, even though she was.

It was around 5:30 in the morning. The street was cold and eerie with little life other than that of the handful of other lone joggers and dog walkers. Sophia began to jog down the pavement. She jogged along three blocks, past houses, a petrol station, a church and her old high school, before she reached the entrance of her local park. She dodged out of the way of an elderly man who was walking out with his old and sad looking golden retriever. The dog instantly began to bark at her, angry and ferocious like a raging fire.

'Sorry,' Sophia apologised underneath her breath as she looked down at the ground, ashamed and afraid, avoiding any eye contact with this stranger and his dog. The dog continued to bark viciously at her for coming too close to his master as she scurried, moving further away from them and from any confrontation that could have come of it. The old man ignored her but the dog's barking was persistent as it growled angrily at Sophia, threatening her with its sharp, claw like teeth. The man had been trying to pull at the dogs' leash, embarrassed and keen to keep walking.

She jogged through the gates of the park and stopped at a bench just inside the entrance to tighten her laces, skimming around at the same time to see if anyone else was there. As usual, like any other Sunday morning, not one single being was to be seen. Three empty cans of Budweiser were stood on the floor beside the bench, making her wary as she looked around, cautious and paranoid in case the culprit was still hanging around. Nobody was there.

Sophia began to jog down a wide path with mountains of golden brown leaves that had been swept to the sides. The park was beautiful and came to life with the vibrant colours of autumn. Trees stood tall and proud every two meters down the path on both the left and right of her. The fields behind them were spotted with evergreen bushes and more trees holding on to what they had left of their red and gold leaves. It was perfection at its finest.

The whole park was the most peaceful and positive place to be in and the perfect place for Sophia to escape. Escape from all of her problems, her nightmares, reality. Everything would disappear, except the voices inside her head as they continued to abuse the drugs from the overflowing coffee cup, addicted to the demonic energy being served within.

Sophia jogged along a sandy footpath that went through a woodland area of tall trees, long grass and bushy hedges.

'Get away.' 'Get out.' 'Go.' The voices inside Sophia's head began to mutter, getting louder and sharper like an angry and violent windstorm. She ignored the tornado that was beginning to form inside her and jogged past a children's playground area, and up a hilly slope that sat further away from the playground, overlooking the nicer part of town.

'You did this, Sophia.' The howling inside her head began to turn into a storm, forming angry flashes of lightening into her soul, creating a burning fire within. But she took no notice, she was nearly there. She jogged down the hill and approached a large pond with a fountain in the middle that sat at the end of the park, not too far from the hilly slope. Opposite the pond was Lilly's, a small and cosy café hidden deep inside the park. She continued to jog around the pond, slowing down her pace as the sounds of the fountain sprinkled into her ears. She was there. The sounds began to drown out the voices that had been hissing at her from inside her head, extinguishing the fire that had been created by the intensity of the caffeine induced storm. There was something about the sound of running water that made Sophia feel at peace. It surrounded her with a sense of harmony giving her the warm hug that she'd been yearning for. She was exhausted. She was tired of running in the park, in her sleep, away from everything throughout her entire life. But she needed this run, it was one with a purpose. A purpose she was yet to figure out.

Just over an hour had passed and Sophia had run over fifteen laps around the park before she decided to head back home. She'd been running almost every day for nearly seven months, but fifteen laps was a new accomplishment for her. Yet she didn't feel a sense of achievement. The closer the man with the blurred face got to her in her nightmares, the more laps around the park she would do out of fear and panic, running away from her problems and the negativity that came with it. Fifteen laps wasn't something to be proud of, it was a sign of failure. Her failure.

Sophia walked, slowly and out of breath towards the same gates that she had entered through. Puffs of condensation left her mouth as she exhaled. She wanted to get back into bed. She was tired, drained and in need of rest but she couldn't let herself fall asleep. She knew the impact of drifting off, she couldn't risk it. Wrestling against tiredness to stay awake and being tortured by the voices inside her head were far more appealing than the effects of falling asleep.

As she walked closer towards the exit, a sudden feeling of uneasiness filled her gut. Everything seemed off and the air had become colder and bitter. A sudden gust of wind struck her face startling the voices inside her head as they began to scream. The sounds tore through her skin like shards of glass being thrown at her in masses. Sophia stopped dead in her tracks. She stood there, terrified and numb. Someone was there, watching her. The figure sat in the distance, on the bench where she'd tightened her laces. He sat, in his muddy blue jeans and his unzipped, dark brown bomber jacket over a navy blue hoodie. His face was down but his eyes were on her, staring at her, watching her.

Uncomfortable, confused and scared, Sophia was loyal to her fears. She froze as her brain refused to communicate with the rest of her body. Her legs became heavy and her meerkat survival tactic had failed her before she could even attempt to run. She kept her eyes on this figure. He was observing her, watching her. The fine hairs on the back of her neck rose as terror struck her soul. Her muscles became tense. She wanted to run but had become paralysed to the spot. The voices inside her head screamed at her to move but she remained stationary. Her mind became clouded with fear. There was nothing she could do. Sophia was weak. He watched her as she stood there, trying to fight the battle with herself.

Adrenaline activated her nervous system as the sound of her heart pounding into her ears became louder and louder. Her blood began to pump through her body viciously bringing her back from her numbness. The man was still watching. It was fight or flight. The voices inside her head began to panic, awakening her meerkat instincts – flight. She began to move, scurrying to the side making sure there was going to be enough space between herself and this man. She had to pass him to get out of the park, she had to be quick, she had to escape. Her legs were heavy as a strong magnetic force began to pull them down towards the ground, making it harder for her to get away. The happenings of her nightmares were becoming real. Her paranoia kicked in and she panicked.

'Who is he?' 'Why is he here?' 'What does he want?' The voices inside her head began to scream at her all at once. 'This is your fault, Sophia.' 'Why are you running?' 'You'll be dead soon.' The nastiness of the voices terrified her. They screamed suddenly with no warning, biting away chunks of her soul each time, making her feel unsafe and unstable in her own body. She sped up, trying to get away from the man, from the voices, from herself. Her large, lion like eyes filled with fear as she continued to feel his eyes piercing through her skin. She couldn't see his face, she didn't look long enough, hard enough. Her goal, for that moment, was to get out of the park, alive. She was a few meters from the gate, but so was he. Sophia sped up and with each step and each skip of her heartbeat, found herself running. She could see him, from the side of her eye as he began to rise from the bench, slowly, face down, eyes still on her.

'Shit!' she whispered to herself as her heart pumped rapidly inside her chest. The meerkat scurried, heading towards the gates, towards this man, hoping she'd get there first.

'Yo!'

A voice called from behind her but she wasn't going to stop. It wasn't real, it wasn't happening, no-one was going to save her. Sophia knew only she could save herself. She wished someone was there to help her, but it wasn't real. She continued to run convincing herself that there was no-one there to help, that it was the voices inside her head, that it was all her imagination. But the man was still there, walking forwards, watching her, waiting.

She ran, away from the voice, away from this strange man, and out of the park gates. She ran down the street with her heart still pumping recklessly. She ran until she was at a safe distance, away from the park, until she was ready to slow down. Still nervous and scared, Sophia turned around. Her entire body was numb with fear. The man was gone. Sophia had escaped, just like in her nightmares. But she hadn't won, and she knew it. This man was still hunting her, teasing her, preparing to move in. Did her nightmare just become real? Sophia was screwed. Whether she was awake or asleep, he was there, and there was nothing she could do. She scurried home. Sophia, the meerkat.

CHAPTER **TWO**

Sophia came home to an empty and silent house. She was shaking, cold and sweaty, in shock and disbelief that this man from her nightmare was now real. She forced herself up the stairs. Her body felt heavy and lifeless as she held on to the bannister tightly, pulling herself up with each step. She entered the bathroom, locking the door behind her, paranoid. She stood at the basin, facing herself in the mosaic mirror. Strands of her hair were stuck to the layer of sweat on her face and neck, and her cheeks had been bitten by the cold wind, covering them in red blotches. She looked away from her reflection, ashamed of the weak and pathetic person that had been staring back at her. She didn't understand what was happening. Nothing made sense, she didn't want it to. She picked up the mirror and looked closer at each of the tiles and cracks, avoiding her reflection. She began to push away the happenings of the morning, tucking them inside the box and closing the lid tightly.

'The bigger picture,' she whispered to herself as her lips spread across her face, remembering the moment when Oliver had given her the mirror. It was during their younger years in their last year of sixth form, back when they were just friends.

***

It was summer 2000, and the final season of the town's Fit to Purpose Football Scheme. It was an incentive put in place by the local council to encourage young students to engage with other six forms and colleges within the borough. Seven teams would be selected to participate in a series of games over the summer period. They'd be invited to attend networking events that helped them focus on team building and communication, preparing them for further education or employment. Over the years, the scheme proved successful and was highly supported by the town's residents and businesses as well as students, teachers and parents.

Totham Sixth Form Football Club had made it through to the final, but had just lost against their superiors, Longpark Sixth Form Football Club. One of the strongest members of the Totham Sixth Form Football Club had missed the goal that led to their defeat against their opponents, leaving the team and their fans feeling let down with the final score.

On-lookers and supporters of the teams were leaving the football stands, some cheerfully and others, disappointed. Sophia, Oliver and their two other friends, Tristan and Lucy, were sitting at the stands discussing the poor outcome of the game as they waited for the grounds to empty out before getting up themselves.

'It can't have been that hard, the goal keeper wasn't even close by,' Tristan had said.

Tristan was one of the most passionate and competitive of the group. He was a typical ladies man; tall, dark and handsome. He was on the strong side, physically and mentally and was never afraid to speak his mind. He was nice and funny, and received a lot of female attention compared to his male companions, including Oliver. Nearly all the girls that crossed his path found something they liked in him other than his appearance. But Tristan had never been interested in relationships, nor was he ever interested in hanging out with the cool kids. Attention was something he didn't welcome and this put off many girls from trying to push too hard to befriend him.

'Yeah, he's not as good as I thought he was. Why is he even allowed to play?' said Lucy, their petite, four-eyed friend. 'It was an open goal, so easy!'

Lucy and Tristan loved to banter with each other. They both had a similar sense of humour that others would describe as spiteful and dark, but they were both genuinely good people. Lucy was the opposite of Sophia, she was strong-minded and bold, and too much to handle for some, but she was never intentionally nasty to anyone. She spoke to everyone, always laughing and joking with people but only truly showed her real self to her close friends. Sophia, Oliver and Tristan were the only people who knew who Lucy really was.

'I bet he wants to kick himself!' she continued.

'Ha! I bet he'd miss that too, Vel.' Tristan followed. Tristan had given Lucy the nick-name earlier in the year after she'd come back from the hair dresser in hysterics because her hair was cut too short. Her thick glasses and height of 4'9 together with the brunette bob reminded him of Velma from the mid-1990s cartoon, *Scooby Doo*, except unlike the real Velma, Lucy definitely wasn't the brains of the group.

She giggled. 'Well, I'll kick him then!'

Sophia smirked a little. Lucy didn't have an ounce of violence in her.

'Erm, excuse me, *I'm* the funny one here, not you!' Tristan laughed at the thought of Lucy kicking anyone.

They always bounced off each other and they'd say everything with a smile, but their smiles faded as Oliver began to stand from his seat. He stepped up onto the seat in front, positioning himself higher than his friends, giving him the feeling of power and authority. Sophia smiled as Lucy and Tristan cheered him on, sarcastically, knowing what was coming.

'Come on then Ol, give it to us,' Tristan teased rubbing his hands together, faking a hunger for hearing what Oliver had to say. Oliver was always the one who tried to settle things, to turn their debates around by introducing different perceptions to their thoughts, even when they were messing around.

He stood on the chair, like a teacher ready to give his pupils some lessons on life. He cleared his throat whilst brushing his soft, shiny hair away from his face, revealing his vibrant, olive skin.

'All I want to say, is that he'd never have scored that goal from where he was. The wind wasn't on his side and neither were the rest of the team. No-one was open for a pass, no-one from his own team were even near the goal.' He looked making eye contact with each of them to make sure they were listening. 'If he was able to pass the damn ball to someone, maybe it would have been a different story.' Oliver paused as he pushed back his hair again, but it slid back into its original position, perfectly framing his delicate yet stubbly face. 'He gave it a shot regardless, and missed. At least he tried, don't knock him for that. He tried.'

Oliver was passionate in his speeches. Sometimes he'd get through and other times he wouldn't, but when he did, he loved seeing their faces as they came to the realisation that they were just being narrow-minded and judgemental. One thing Oliver couldn't listen to was the foul and negative judgements of one person against another.

Tristan and Lucy mumbled beneath their breath.

'Still, it was an open goal,' said Lucy, who loved to

debate, but more out of bitchiness than from facts or anything else. As much as she loved him, she couldn't stand Oliver's continued efforts of preaching his lifestyle and thoughts onto the rest of them.

He stepped back down with a smug look on his face and carried on saying words they didn't want to hear.

'Well, I suggest you try and take a shot from that distance Vel, with all of us watching and shouting, and if, or when you score, maybe then you can say that.'

Lucy looked at Tristan and rolled her eyes, evidently for Oliver to see. Oliver ignored his que to shut up and continued to make his point.

'He tried Vel. What you see, and what I see are two different things. You shouldn't take things only for what you see in front of you. Step back and look at the bigger picture, even then you probably won't know the full story, but you'll be able to get a bit closer to seeing it as it is. You just need to look and…'

Lucy glanced sideways, turning her head away from Oliver, clenching her teeth and taking a deep breath at the same time. She hated being challenged or called out, especially by Oliver, who had a reputation of handing out more than his fair share of his opinion.

'…be open,' he finished.

Lucy pulled down her eyebrows as they sunk behind her thick glasses. Her lips tightened. She looked up at Oliver, even more annoyed at his inability to read signs, for not knowing when to stop, for being so obsessed with spreading his beliefs like the feelings or judgements of anyone else never existed. Lucy knew all about the bigger picture that he preached. She'd spent most of her life being judged for being the way she was by people who didn't know her. Oliver's words would sometimes open up the wounds of her past that she would rather not give any attention. His words would pierce through the sections of her brain where she'd locked away all of the badness, releasing them little by little, bringing them to light as he pushed the knife further inside. The blood would drip for days and it would take even longer for the cuts to scar over. And then he'd do it all over again, opening up her wounds, stopping her from healing. He hoped that one day, she'd be able to let go of her bad memories instead of imprisoning them inside her body. Everything he did, he did out of love, although not everybody saw it that way.

Despite their constant arguments and disagreements, Lucy loved him. She saw Oliver like a brother. She knew him the longest out of everyone in their group but was the only one who was so easily irritated by him. He knew what annoyed her, and he'd use it to his advantage, lovingly.

'Okay, no-one cares Ol.' Tristan interrupted, knowing it was about to get heated given the look on Lucy's face. Tristan couldn't be bothered to listen to another one of Oliver and Lucy's disagreements. It had been a nice day, but it was time to leave.

The stands had emptied out and the football ground was a lot quieter. Oliver picked up his rucksack from the floor and flung it across his shoulder as he slipped his arm through one of the straps. The others picked up their bags too in preparation to call it a day and head home.

'It is what it is.' Oliver never let Lucy's reactions get the worst of him.

Sophia smiled. It was her only involvement in the whole conversation. She loved hearing about his views. She liked his mannerism and the way he looked at life. He saw things nobody else did and he bought light into their conversations and turned them into educational debates or lessons. At least she thought so anyway.

Lucy headed away from the football stands and towards the gates to exit the grounds, ensuring there was a distance between herself and Oliver. Tristan sped up to catch up with her whilst Sophia and Oliver walked together not too far behind. The breeze had picked up, a little stronger and cooler than before. Sophia walked with her arms crossed as an attempt to keep herself warm. Lucy sped up, cold and wanting to get home quicker. Neither of them had a cardigan or coat, and neither of the boys offered theirs.

As they walked, Sophia asked Oliver to elaborate on his previous conversation with Lucy. She enjoyed listening to his positivity. His words would drown out some of her thoughts and remove the negativity and sadness that she had hidden within her from her own past, even if it was for a short moment.

'Think about it Soph.' Oliver smiled. 'It's a game. We're all watching, hundreds of people are watching. He didn't wake up to want to fail. It takes a lot to take chances, especially when you're going it alone when everyone else is counting on you and you know the likeliness of scoring isn't even 50/50.' He stopped to put on his rucksack properly. 'That's not just a game of football Soph.' He slipped his arm through the strap and continued to walk on. 'That's life. People are always watching, waiting for you to fail so they can say something. They will knock you when things go wrong, when you do something wrong, without looking at the bigger picture.' He'd spoken with so much passion about the mind, about perception, choices and chances. He continued, leaving her mesmerised through each word he uttered. 'Rather to have tried and have it go wrong than to not have tried at all. Mistakes are made by people every single day.' They slowed down as they began to approach Sophia's house. 'You don't know anyone's reason for making the choices they make. You can't always get it right, but you learn from it in one way or another. Good or bad. Let it be. Let it go. I'm sure he knows himself what he's done wrong, who are we to sit there and tell him, to make him feel any more low and worthless than he probably already feels?' Oliver swiped his hair from across his face as the breeze pulled it back forward.

Sophia was confused, wondering how the topic had steered into something else other than a friendly game of football. She knew he had previous setbacks and traumatic experiences in his childhood, but she assumed he had overcome them. She wondered whether he was having difficulties in letting go of his own past, whether he was using Lucy as a scapegoat for his issues. No. Not Oliver. She brushed it off. Oliver was fine.

'It is what it is,' he continued.

They came to a stop as they stood outside Sophia's house. Sophia lived the closest to the sixth form, around a three minute walk away. The others didn't live too far. Tristan lived the furthest which was still only a twenty minute walk. He lived on the nicer part of town, on the other side of the local park where the streets and houses seemed a lot larger and spacious.

'Peace out, Soph!' Tristan stuck his arm up in the air as he and Lucy continued to walk on ahead. Oliver stopped beside Sophia to take the opportunity to finish what he was saying, ignoring the goosebumps on her naked arms. He loved the sound of his voice.

'To cut a long story short, what I'm trying to say, is that nothing is just either black or white. Every colour has a variety of shades, and each shade is different depending on who is looking at it and what it's against. People shouldn't have the right to say what is and what isn't right or wrong. And people shouldn't mock others for taking chances and making choices.' Oliver turned to face Sophia as he held on to each of the rucksack straps as though he was sitting on a rollercoaster. The eager look in her eyes, the calmness in her face and the silence of her breath told him to continue as she hid her cold shivers beneath her skin.

'Be it right or wrong, there's a reason behind every choice a person has made. Sometimes it's the right choice, sometimes it's the wrong choice, and sometimes their decisions can't be justified as time moves on. But no-one has a right to judge.' Oliver paused as he fought the breeze, pushing back his hair, sweeping it to one side of his head and holding it in place. 'At the same time, people should focus on their own self. The only person they need to think about improving or being better than is the person they see in the mirror, using their own reflection to see the bigger picture, in themselves, not in anyone else. That's where it starts.' He stepped back and turned his body away from Sophia, still facing her. 'It's all about educating people on self-realisation, that's all,' he winked at her. 'Catch you later Soph.'

Oliver was a man of many words, but he also practised what he preached and never judged anyone. Teaching kindness was Oliver's passion and he spoke of it whenever he had the chance. Sophia smiled and nodded as Oliver turned and began walking away, waving one arm in the air as he took large strides to catch up to Tristan and Lucy, who had drastically slowed down their pace for him. Sophia watched him walk off, with his red and orange rucksack that bounced with each step, over his thin, bright green hooded jumper, with washed blue jeans and tan coloured trainers. He was smart and he was wise but one thing he didn't have, was a sense of fashion. She smiled and turned toward her front door.

It wasn't until the following morning outside her English class when Oliver had presented her with a box.

'So yesterday, sorry if it got a bit intense,' Oliver began. 'But this is where the bigger picture starts.' He handed her a small box. Inside was a fine little mosaic mirror, with blue and green tiles around the edges, shiny and sparkly. Sophia smiled. It was the first time Oliver had given her anything. They'd been friends for just over seven years but this year, the final year of sixth form, was different.

***

She stood in the bathroom and stared at her reflection in the mirror. She smiled as she reminisced about Oliver's charm, his way with words, how mesmerised she was by him, how she would get lost in the beauty of his eyes each time he spoke.

She placed the mirror back on the shelf and untied her hair, pushing it back as she peeled away the strays that had been stuck to her face. She tied it back up in a messy bun before washing the sweat from her face while glaring back into the mirror. It was a lot more than just a mirror. No matter how many cracks, dents and chips it had on it today, and no matter how much the colour had faded from the tiles, to Sophia this mirror still sparkled the same way it had done when she first received it, and it still carried the same message as it did seventeen years ago. She smiled at herself and left the bathroom, drying her face while making her way down the stairs.

It had been a long day already and it was only just gone 7:00 a.m. Sophia put the kettle on before making her way into the living room. She perched herself on the armrest of a white, leather sofa, waiting for the kettle to boil. She sat there, trying to make sense of everything that had been happening over the past few days, months even. She sat there, thinking about her nightmares, the man in the park, everything that had begun to haunt her. Maybe it was time to talk to Oliver. She couldn't. She couldn't bring herself to understand the truth as she pushed back more unwanted happenings from her mind. Oliver was out on his own walk, his own escape. Sophia decided it was a sign not to tell him about the strange man in the park, there was no need.

Going out for a jog alone meant facing some of her biggest fears, and it was just one of the many steps she'd taken as an attempt to become stronger.

A loud bang came from the hallway, startling Sophia, who had frozen instantly. Another sign reminding her that she was weak. The sound came again, bursting its way through the hallway and into her ears. Someone was at the front door, knocking. She could feel her heart begin to race as it thumped inside her chest. Another knock echoed through the hallway. Sophia's mind was exhausted and drained with fear from all of the happenings of the morning. Was this real? She was confused. She didn't need this. Another knock erupted into her ears as she imagined the door being ripped from its hinges. She had to stay silent, but each beat of her heart became louder and louder as it pounded violently against her chest. Another two knocks slammed against the front door, this time louder than the ones before. Sophia walked towards the window, slowly, shaking nervously. Another knock. The sound came booming into the room, drowning out the drums of her heartbeat, deafening her instantly. She took a deep breath and stopped in front of the window, hiding behind the curtains as she peeped outside, trying to remain unseen like the lion that she was supposed to be, before pouncing on her prey, shredding it to pieces and tearing into it limb from limb. But she was a meerkat. She stood, hiding away, trying not to be seen as she watched a tall man standing at the top of the steps, shuffling on his feet as he waited for her to let him in. Sophia exhaled and relaxed her body as she walked back to the sofa. She sat down, ignoring the man outside. She lay back, making herself comfortable. She closed her eyes, zoning herself out, back to the good days when she was in sixth form.

The man was still outside.

CHAPTER THREE

'Thank you,' Sophia smiled at Oliver, appreciative of her sparkly new mirror. The sentiment and meaning behind the mosaic mirror made it that much more special. She herself was very sentimental. Things meant so much more to her when they were personal and had real thought behind them, compared to gifts that were focused on their monetary value, which, to her, were generally just replaceable objects.

Oliver nodded and returned a smile. 'Enjoy your class Soph,' he winked and began to walk off.

'Oh Oli, I forgot to say,' Sophia called him back. She waited for him to turn around before continuing. 'Tristan's birthday. My last lesson is at 2:45 today. I'm going into town afterwards to grab a few bits for him.' She was the worst when it came to getting to the point and asking people for anything.

Oliver smiled, amused at her failed attempt at

asking for a contribution to Tristan's birthday present. Even though they all did it for each other every year, Sophia struggled to ask.

'No problem, Soph. I'll add a ten.' He pulled out his wallet from his back pocket and began looking through the little compartments that were all filled with bits of paper, receipts and cards, in search for a ten pound note. He'd been scuffling around in his wallet for what seemed to be at least three long minutes. 'It's me being blind. Too much rubbish in here, give me a sec, I know I didn't spend it.' Oliver continued to search his wallet. 'Okay, maybe you'll do a better job.' He handed over his wallet to Sophia.

As calm and gentle as she was, one thing Sophia lacked was patience and Oliver was well aware of it. She placed her new mirror and its box on the window sill in the corridor, and took Oliver's overly cluttered wallet from him. As she rummaged through the random receipts and pieces of paper, she came across a small, worn and tatty piece of card, folded up at least three times into a little rectangle. Sophia pulled it out of the wallet, intrigued and wanting a closer look. She was curious. She looked at Oliver, using her eyes to ask him if it was okay to take a peek. He looked back, tightening up his shoulders, feeling uneasy. Sophia smiled. Oliver watched her eyes glisten through her smile and he said 'yes' by exchanging nothing but a smile back.

Sophia had been careful not to tear this fragile piece of card. She knew Oliver well enough to know that this was more than just an old, scruffy piece of card. It had become so worn it may have well been a piece of paper. She knew it was something that held a lot of sentimental value to him. She unfolded it gently, three times as it grew into a long, thin strip that stretched across thirty centimetres. The words 'Live each day as if it were your last,' were handwritten across the top in black, capital letters. Underneath the heading, along the centre of the page was a long line with various numbers and more words. Oliver had outlined his lifetime goals onto this thirty centimetre strip of card in the form of a timeline, starting from the age of thirteen and ending at forty with the words 'Part 1 of 2' written on the bottom right hand corner.

Sophia studied the timeline.

Age 13, set my goals, age 16, study hard and get into sixth form, age 18, start a career, age 20, travel and explore, books, cultures, people, the world, age 28, get married and buy a house, by 30, have at least two children, age 31, make a start on writing my novel…

'It's my 'to do' list, bucket list, life goals.' Oliver interrupted Sophia's focus, feeling the need to explain what it was that she was looking at despite it being obvious. 'Whatever you want to call it,' he looked down, almost as though he was embarrassed. Sophia looked up and smiled at him in amazement, feeling uncomfortable with his reaction to her seeing it.

'That's pretty impressive Ol,' she welcomed him to tell her more.

'It's everything in one,' he continued, his voice still low, still half unsure whether he should go on.

Teaching life lessons, positivity, and raising self-awareness within others was one thing, but when it came to speaking of himself and his own goals, Oliver was never comfortable, for no reason other than because no-one had ever asked him or been interested in what he wanted.

Sophia smiled again, kindly and warmly, taking a closer look at the tatty piece of paper in her hands. Her interaction encouraged him to speak openly.

'And it's always with me. I know what my focus is, I know where I was, where I am, where I'm going,' he raised his head to look at her.

Sophia was amazed. She'd known Oliver since her first year of high school and throughout sixth form but had never seen this side to him before. She was aware he had dreams and goals, and future ideas like most people, but he always seemed shy to talk about it. She'd never seen anyone so obsessed and passionate about life, about having goals and actually doing something about it and taking precautions to meet them. She was so used to being around people who lived only by the cards they were dealt with, accepting where they were in life and just doing what they needed to do, rather than setting targets and taking the steps to shape their own future. She didn't know of any other way of living, and never thought there would be any other option than just to keep walking down the path she was put on.

'I know it's battered. I've had it for years.' Oliver was embarrassed of its state, but eventually felt pleased to have shown it to her, even if it was unintentional. He'd kept this tiny piece of card in his wallet for nearly six years, a timeline, laying out his life plans of tomorrow. Sophia saw how much this little card meant to him. She stood there, examining this ancient looking document in her hands. She felt proud of him, happy for him and inspired by who and how he was. He was indeed, a good person with an extremely beautiful soul.

'Can I give this back to you later on?' Sophia asked as she gently began folding it back into the original state that she found it in.

Oliver hesitated.

'I promise you'll get it back soon, before I head off for the day.' She looked at his face, at the uneasiness of letting go of something he'd held on to for so many years, even if it was just for a few hours. The nervousness was evident through his eyes and all the signs on his face and across his body screamed 'no'.

Sophia smiled and raised an eyebrow. Her eyes shone and sparkled as she looked up at him. Once again, Oliver agreed almost instantly, with a beautiful smile right back at hers.

'Catch you later,' he said as he walked away smiling and feeling slightly weird at the same time. No-one had ever asked Oliver to talk about his goals before. He felt good.

It was just before 9:00 a.m. and the first lesson for the day was about to begin. Oliver didn't have a lesson for another two hours but always went in early regardless. Most students who didn't have 9:00 a.m. starts didn't really step into the building until they had their first lesson. Yet Oliver was different. He liked routine. Of course there were times where he didn't mind doing spur of the moment things, but eighty percent of the time he needed to know what he was going to do and when he was going to do it. He always needed to be in control of where his life was heading, despite knowing well that there was only so much of it he could actually control at the same time. Despite this, the overall intention of building his own path was always there.

Sophia put the little timeline into the pocket of her jeans before picking up the mirror and its box from the window sill. She walked into the classroom, towards her desk and sat down, placing the mirror back into the box and carefully into her bag. She'd been smiling to herself, feeling content and grateful for having someone like Oliver around.

Oliver and Tristan were the only two men in her life. Sophia's dad had left her and her mum, Isabella, when Sophia was just eleven. He was a good man with good values and he loved and cherished his family, staying loyal and truthful right until the end. He'd broken one promise in his life, one so painful that Sophia never could forgive or accept. He'd always promised he'd be there for his queen and his princess whenever they needed him. It was the one promise Sophia needed him to keep, and the one promise he'd broken. On March 14 1993, he stopped by the grocery store on his way home from work to pick up a box of chocolates for Sophia's eleventh birthday. He was stabbed in the chest for nothing other than for being in the wrong place at the wrong time. He had died instantly.

It was a tragedy that no-one had expected, and one that neither Sophia nor Isabella got over. Whenever she was surrounded by silence, the voices inside her head would tell her that she was to blame for his death, that her birthday was an evil day and that she carried bad luck with her wherever she went. Sophia had seen all the heartbreak and pain in the world through her mums suffering because of it and it never left either of them. She promised herself that she would never get into the same situation as her mum, one where she'd love someone unconditionally, so much that it would destroy her if he were to leave. Her mums' words were ingrained in her, constantly reminding Sophia that she should never allow herself to fall in love or give anyone the power of making her cry to a point where she'd lose herself enough to drown in her own tears. Isabella would always tell Sophia to never let anyone hurt her enough to bring a tear to her eyes, and Sophia would listen.

She'd stuck by it ever since, not letting anyone

make her cry. But she'd make herself cry every night when no-one was there to see. Her methods of coping with pain and hurt were simply kept a secret. She'd bottle up her feelings from people and run away, hiding in her bed, turning her into the meerkat she was today.

Sophia reached for the timeline from her pocket and bent down to her bag again, placing the timeline inside the box with the mosaic mirror to avoid causing any more damage to it. The thought of Oliver made her feel happy inside. She smiled.

'Erm, Soph. Don't be so rude!' Lucy had emerged out of nowhere and nudged Sophia in disgust. Sophia jolted slightly, in shock and shook her head with no expression on her face other than confusion. Up until that moment she'd been oblivious to her surroundings. The room was packed with twenty eight other students all talking at once to one another and yet prior to Lucy nudging her, she'd heard nothing.

'So did you?' Lucy asked.

'Did I what?' Sophia was still blank.

'Damn woman, what's up with you? Did you watch *The Walking Dead* last night? It was actually one of the best ones yet!' Lucy went on without waiting for an answer. 'So basically, I'll tell you what happened, so Negan, wait, do want to know? You're not going to watch it are you?'

Lucy loved watching TV programmes in the evenings and spent most of the day telling everyone what happened in them regardless of whether they watched them or not, and regardless of whether they were interested or not. TV was Lucy's life and her own way of escaping from her reality.

'Saved!' Sophia laughed as Mr. Barkley, their English teacher, walked into the classroom. She didn't care about *The Walking Dead* or any other TV programme in fact, other than *Friends* – the one thing that made her smile after her dad had passed.

'Whatever! I'll tell you later.' Lucy walked to her desk as the rest of the class settled down and made their way to theirs.

Today, they were to continue their lesson on *The Lord of the Flies* by William Golding, a book about a group of school boys who are stranded on an island following a plane crash. There are no surviving adults, and so the boys behave like any other human would in a place without rules, letting the stronger of their two different characteristics take over; setting and obeying the rules of civilisation versus the human impulse to power and savagery. It was one of Sophia's favourite books. They were on chapter five and Mr. Barkley had read a passage. One of the lines stood out to Sophia about fear and dreams. It reminded her of a conversation about commitment and relationships between herself and Oliver earlier in the year, when she'd told him she was afraid of getting into one after what she'd witnessed between her own parents. He'd told her that it was fear that stopped people from living.

'Fear ends up causing the most amount of hurt and regret later on in life, but by then it might be too late. Letting fear hurt you is your own choice. Anything can happen in a dream, but nothing actually happens. You can wake up from a dream. Fear is the same. You can be afraid, and nothing will happen. Fear makes you stop, but time waits for no-one.'

There were many things that Oliver had said to Sophia, but those words stuck. 'Fear makes you stop, but time waits for no-one.' Even if she wasn't aware of it in that moment, it was these little talks and phrases that she would remember forever, and it was these little conversations that would keep her going, giving her the strength she needed to move away from the voices inside her head.

'Oliver would love this book,' she thought to herself, with a slight hint of a smile stretching across her face. Sophia looked away quickly, feeling slightly embarrassed, wondering why she'd even thought of Oliver just then in the first place. They were friends.

After forty five minutes of reading and analysing the chapter in more detail, their lesson was over. The murmur of students talking loudened as they got up from their seats, packing their books away and continuing the conversations they were having prior to Mr. Barkley walking in. Luckily for Sophia, Lucy had forgotten about *The Walking Dead*. They made their way to the community area of the school where some of the sixth form students hung out during their free time.

The area didn't have a tremendous amount of space compared to the number of students that were in the sixth form, but it was big enough to accommodate the handful of students who did use it. It was a rectangular room with walls filled with lime green and navy blue paint. The room was split into two sections; one equipped with tables, chairs and computers for those who wanted to study, and the other for those who wanted to use their free time relaxing on the bright orange sofas or playing on the foosball table in the corner of the room. There was also a door to a smaller, quieter room, known as the 'Silent Study' which was usually empty.

Sophia and Lucy walked into the community area and scanned the room before spotting Oliver and Tristan both engrossed in Tristan's phone whilst sitting on the sofa side by side.

'Sup,' said Lucy as she approached them, showing acknowledgement of their presence rather than posing a question to actually wanting to know how they were.

'Hey.' Sophia followed with a smile. She was calm, shy and reserved, despite having known them for such a long time.

They both stood in front of Oliver and Tristan, indicating for them to move apart so they could plant themselves onto the sofa in between them. Tristan had been playing a game on his phone and Oliver had been watching him lose. The girls had arrived at the right time.

'Still trying to beat my score? Get off your phone T, Oli's bored of watching you hurt yourself like that. You can't beat my score.' Lucy sat further back into the sofa, making herself comfortable, pushing Tristan and Sophia at the same time as they adjusted to give her more room. 'In fact, you can't beat anyone's score, ever!'

She always teased Tristan. They were both so competitive at everything. Lucy would always win when it came to games and Tristan wouldn't ever accept it. It all started after he'd let her win at a game of arm wrestling one time and she gloated, telling people she'd won against him. But whenever he'd challenge her to a rematch in front of an audience, she'd refuse. Since then, he refused to let her, or anyone else, win at anything. But he was never really good at playing games.

'Damn. How much space do you need Vel? There are three other people on this sofa you know, and you're the smallest.' Tristan moved into Lucy, taking back his space while compressing her like a sandwich between himself and Sophia.

'If you're not comfortable then move, you've been sitting here for long enough.' Lucy pushed him back.

'Actually, he's only been here for about fifteen minutes.' Oliver interrupted as Tristan sniggered.

'That's still fifteen minutes more than me!' Lucy moved her bum further into the sofa, moving back towards Tristan giving Sophia her space back.

'I feel sorry for your future husband!' Tristan joked

as he stood up. 'Let's hope he's a gentleman like me or your fat ass will never be comfortable!'

Lucy giggled. 'Hey! I could make you my husband if I wanted to!' Lucy said, smiling as she stuck out her leg to kick his. 'But I don't hate you that much and you're just not that lucky!' she laughed.

'That doesn't even make sense but okay Vel.' Tristan kicked her back playfully.

Oliver leaned forward. 'Neither of you can do commitment, isn't that what a relationship is?' Oliver was brilliant at interrupting. Relationship conversations were the ones that annoyed the rest of the group the most.

'Oh! Oh! Here it comes. Nice one Vel!' Tristan laughed and turned his head as he stood by the sofa uncomfortably, still looking down at his phone playing his game.

'Huh?' Lucy looked up at Tristan who had turned away from his phone, waiting for his game to restart after having lost again. Lucy rolled her eyes and began to speak.

'Listen,' she leaned forward on the sofa and turned towards Oliver. 'I've told you again and again, over a hundred times and I'm not going to say it again. I'm entitled to an opinion, and my opinion of a relationship is mine, right or wrong, it's mine. If I don't want to get married and stay with one person for the rest of my life, so what? If that's what you want then good for you Ol, everyone is different remember?'

Oliver had always somehow managed to get into discussions about relationships and it never failed to annoy the rest of the group, who'd witnessed or experienced bad encounters around love and relationships in their past. Oliver's biggest flaw was not learning to let things go.

He continued, 'I just don't understand why. Why wouldn't you want to be around someone you get on with, who knows you, everything about you, who gets you...'

'Right!' Lucy cut Oliver off and sat up straight, eyes forward glaring at the foosball table as if she was ready to go *Hulk* on it. She was never violent but had imagined punching Oliver in the face plenty of times throughout their friendship.

'I've said this before,' she continued. 'Life changes people. I could love someone today but what about in ten years' time? Shit can happen during those ten years. Shit happens and people change because of it. Why force yourself to go down a path with someone who you may not want to walk along with for the rest of your life? Get out of fairy-tale land Mr. Oliver Cane and step into the real world! Nothing lasts forever.'

She'd stood up, trying not to show how annoyed she really was at Oliver's constant attempts to turn her banter into serious life talks, but she was never good at hiding her anger.

'Game, T?' She hadn't even waited for an answer before walking towards the foosball table. Tristan put his phone in his pocket. Another game lost. He gave Oliver a friendly nod as he walked away.

'And he does it again. Well done Oli, you hit a nerve or two there.' Sophia turned to Oliver, straight faced. She and Tristan had stayed silent throughout the whole ordeal. When it came to Oliver and Lucy, it was best to sit back and turn to deaf ears. They'd been friends the longest, since the beginning of primary school in fact, and both had the same after school counselling sessions twice a week too for nearly two years. They fought like brother and sister, but defended each other and had each other's backs if anyone else was to ever say or do anything against the other. It was a mutual understanding between them, that only they could cross the line with each other the way they did. Sophia and Tristan had learned this about their relationship over time and steered clear when they had their moments.

'Obviously, it's not exactly difficult with that one,' he replied.

It was a common thing between them, for Oliver to start some debate he knew Lucy was so passionate about. He'd never do it in a cruel way. He'd always have the intention of trying to get people to tap into another area within their mind and soul, where hope and faith lie, to make them think about their thoughts and why those thoughts were with them. He wanted to make them realise that the bad things that have happened in the past should remain there, left there, in the past. He'd never understood how much people let the negative past affect their present, and ultimately, their future. Most people were all about 'you only live once,' while Oliver truly lived every single day, knowing that in reality, you only die once. He was so passionate about this that he had the words 'Live each day as if it were your last' tattoo-ed on the left side of his chest, above a picture of two hands in prayer. He was also a true believer of God – another topic of debate within the female members of their group.

Of course, Oliver hadn't always been this way. He'd once taken advantage of life, like any normal child. He'd spend his days watching TV, playing games and doing nothing. But at just eleven years old, Oliver was diagnosed with a brain tumour. Years of treatment and fighting changed his views of life forever. He began to understand the importance and value of time and respect for even the smallest of things. He understood that every day people wake up having been given another chance, and yet everyday people refuse to take it. Instead, they would do the same things over and over again, and feel incomplete and unaccomplished. That was what he was trying to teach, despite not always going about it in the right way.

'I get what she's saying Soph, but I've always wanted to be with one person, only one person who is, if I'm lucky, my soulmate. I'd get married to her, have children with her. The thought of waking up to her only and seeing only her face every day, knowing her inside out and she knowing me inside out, knowing the good and bad and still wanting to grow old togeth...'

'Fair enough, but not everyone thinks the same. You know this.' Sophia had to interrupt. Her views weren't too far off from Lucy's and she herself had never wanted commitment either. She never wanted to be close to anyone enough for it to impact her whole life, especially after witnessing what it did to her mum. She'd be stupid if she was to let herself go through the same.

'Just let people think for themselves and make their own decisions and, don't judge anyone just because they don't have the same thoughts and beliefs as you Oli.' Sophia forced a nervous smile across her face before licking her dry lips as they cracked, painting her lips with spots of red. She looked down at her clammy hands, avoiding any eye contact with Oliver. She had been peeling off her baby pink nail varnish from her fingernails. She'd never spoken back to anyone before. She was frustrated with Oliver's pushy stance on relationships, whilst panicking at the same time, surprised at herself for the words that were coming out of her mouth. She never knew she had it in her. Maybe she wasn't a pushover after all.

'You of all people should know better. You preach this whole thing about not judging people and people behaving the way they do for a reason.' Sophia felt the fire inside her. It felt good. 'It's not just either black or white remember? There are other colours.'

She turned her head back to the foosball table, at Lucy and Tristan playing and laughing.

Oliver smiled, honoured to hear his words come out of someone else's mouth, whilst also fascinated and confused at the same time over Sophia's newly found voice. He wasn't sure how he felt about someone like Sophia talking back to him. It wasn't right. Just as he was about to speak, a small ball came flying from across the room. It came in fast and out of nowhere, hitting Sophia right in the centre of her forehead, punishing her for speaking her mind for the first time. Oliver smiled but Sophia didn't see.

Tristan had laughed loudly from the foosball table at the accuracy of how centred it was. If that was the aim of the game, he would definitely have won. Lucy came running over.

'So sorry Soph! He was aiming at Oli's face not yours!' Lucy joked as she grabbed the ball and ran back to the table. Sophia smiled at Lucy's quick little attempt to indirectly curse Oliver before running back to the foosball table. She was also embarrassed to have been hit in the middle of the forehead by a foosball, wondering how she'd not seen it coming, especially when she'd been looking right at it.

Oliver gave Sophia a look of sympathy as he watched her rub her head and look embarrassed at the same time. He looked at her, in a different way to how he had ever looked at her before. His dark eyes sparkled with so much beauty. He looked at her with care, in a more than friends sort of way. His pupils were dilated, large and shiny as they stared at her, sending her messages through these glass mirrors, sending her vibes, connections. Sophia could feel it too.

'Do you want anything from the vending machine?' Sophia stood up from the sofa and grabbed her bag as she turned to Oliver, who was still seated, now with the whole sofa to himself.

'I'm actually okay thanks,' he replied. The moment was awkward, it was clear there was something between them just then, but they both shrugged it off.

'Okay.' Sophia walked away towards the foosball table, asking Lucy and Tristan if they'd wanted anything before making her way out of the room.

She had disappeared for nearly twenty minutes before coming back with a Bounty for herself, a bar of Crunchie for Oliver and two packs of Malteasers, one for Lucy and the other for Tristan.

'Make these from scratch? You've been gone long enough.' Lucy and Tristan were back on the sofa with Oliver now. The atmosphere was back to normal between them. Lucy had clearly won that game of foosball against Tristan, and Sophia had been lucky enough to avoid having to hear twenty minutes of banter between them.

'Oh damn!' Tristan jumped from the sofa. He was late for his maths class. He grabbed his bag and pack of Malteasers, waving it up in the air at Sophia as he walked away. 'Cheers Soph! Peace.' He disappeared out of the room.

Tristan was talented. He had many interests and gave his all in everything he did. He was the most academic of their group and had been encouraged by his parents to focus on his education and his dreams from a young age. He'd been sent to tuition once a week from the age of six right through to sixteen, and had later finished his GCSEs, passing with six A+s and four As. He'd never show his intelligence outside of his exams and lessons however, and other than his close friends and family, no-one really knew how smart he actually was. He'd always been seen playing games on his phone, at the foosball table or hanging out by the football pitches during or after sixth form even though games and sport were his weaknesses. But he'd never missed a lesson and at home, he'd study hard. His parents made sure of it. His mum was a lecturer at a nearby university, teaching ancient history, and his dad was a barrister. They were good, hard-working people, genuine, kind and focused. They'd raised Tristan and his younger brother, Ashley, to be the same and every Sunday, they'd volunteer to teach religion to younger students at their local church. He never preached to his friends, who all had their own views of religion, which he respected, and they respected too.

Sophia savoured her Bounty, making herself comfortable on the sofa while Lucy sat quietly, sucking the chocolate off of each Malteaser before allowing the biscuit to bubble and dissolve on her tongue one by one. Oliver put his Crunchie in his bag for later. He never ate chocolate before 12:00 p.m. it was an unspoken rule of his that they all knew about.

'Foosball ladies?' he asked.

Lucy shook her head as she stuck another Malteaser in her mouth and sat further back into the sofa, leaning against Sophia's arm. Oliver wasn't as competitive as Tristan, and she'd always enjoyed a competitive game more compared to one with an ongoing commentary in the background from Oliver about how 'it's all about enjoying yourself, and not about winning.' Right now, she was calm and she wasn't about to let Oliver ruin it.

Sophia felt bad, but turned him down regardless. She wasn't into foosball.

'Tell us about your book,' Sophia turned to Oliver. She showed genuine interest in his random little projects.

'What?' Lucy stuck another Malteaser in her mouth.

'Oli's going to be writing a book.' Sophia looked at Oliver and smiled.

Lucy crunched her Malteaser, fast, and got up. 'Nice. Just saw Ash, be back in a second.' Lucy had gone over towards the Silent Study room to speak to Ashley, Tristan's younger brother. She didn't care about Oliver's book.

Sophia smiled at Oliver, raising her eyebrows as though she had been apologising in case he felt bad by Lucy's reaction. Oliver didn't mind. He knew Lucy didn't intentionally mean to be spiteful.

Sophia moved forward from the sofa and reached for her bag. She rummaged through it before pulling out his little timeline.

'I'm going to go and get Tristan's stuff now while I've got time, so I don't have to go afterwards,' she said whilst handing over the timeline to Oliver. 'I hope you don't mind that I laminated it.' Sophia smiled and walked away.

Oliver had been looking at the laminated timeline, ignoring the words that were coming out of Sophia's mouth unintentionally. He looked down and smiled, not because it was laminated, but because it was Sophia who laminated it. He smiled and shook his head, removing his thoughts of Sophia, and then wondering how he'd never thought to laminate the timeline himself. This timeline meant that little bit more to him now than it did a few hours ago. He smiled again at the thought of Sophia. There was definitely something there.

As the day had gone on, Sophia had trailed off into a trance every now and again, hearing Oliver's speech behind the mosaic mirror, the sound of his laugh, and seeing his deeply set, marble-like eyes glisten every time he smiled. Everything she saw and every conversation she had with anyone began to remind her of him. They'd been friends for nearly seven years, but something else was beginning to appear, something so different and so much stronger than anything else. There had been many moments behind every interaction they had for a few weeks, and it was only getting more obvious and so much clearer each time, that something was happening, something that had never happened to Sophia before. She had to snap out of it. They were friends, best friends. They were BFFs.

CHAPTER **FOUR**

Another knock on the door drowned her thoughts, bringing Sophia back to reality. Her ways of escaping were just temporary. She needed something solid, something to keep her away, forever. Another knock thumped against her ear drums, followed by the sound of a man's voice as it came flooding in through the letter box, imprisoning Sophia in her own home.

'Listen, I know you're in there.'

She knew this voice. It belonged to Tristan - loud, deep, and strong. She wasn't planning on opening the door, nor was she going to talk to him. She knew him well, she knew he'd leave if she stayed silent, but she knew he'd come back too. And that was fine.

'I want to talk to you, you can't run forever,' he tried again.

Yes, she could. She continued to ignore him, like she did a few weeks ago, and a few weeks before that, and she'll ignore him today, and again in a few more weeks, just like she'd been doing for over seven months now.

She stood from the sofa and walked back towards the window. She watched blankly, as he turned to walk down the steps. She was annoyed at how he was still trying to get to her. Was Tristan the man who was calling out to her in the park? She couldn't tell. The sparkle from her eyes turned to dust and the voices inside her head began to wake. She waited until he was out of sight, before she attemped her next temporary escape.

Sophia turned and dragged herself towards the hallway and up the stairs. She walked unusually slowly as she struggled with each step, in a daze and worn out. Fear sat heavy on her heart as the voices inside her head began to whisper. Insanity began to steal her mind like a thief taking away anything good from someone who had been burgled before. She walked into the bathroom and glared at her reflection in the mosaic mirror. She was tired and in desperate need of sleep. She stood, looking at her herself, unable to recognise the person staring back at her. Months of running away and living in anxiousness made it easier for Sophia to become a thin and almost imaginary figure walking across the town. Unseen and unnoticed. But it did nothing for her mind. She remained secluded, free to roam the world, but trapped inside her mind, like being stuck in a prison without any walls.

Sophia moved her body toward the shower and turned on the hot water, letting it run while she undressed. The steam from the water began to create a layer of condensation over the mosaic mirror and bathroom tiles. Sophia waited until her face had faded behind the sheet of dew before stepping into the shower. The heat from the downpour as it touched her skin relaxed her and her shoulders dropped instantly as she allowed herself to cry. Her tears merged within the stream of water that flowed from the showerhead, down her face and body before escaping into the drain. She stood there, under this monsoon of rain, letting out every emotion inside her. Pain, anger, fear, her lack of focus and the loss of will to carry on, left her body. She cried, hopelessly until she felt the weight of her emotions leave her soul. She cried as she watched it all wash away and disappear, deep into the drain. But she knew it was temporary. It was less than twenty four hours until she'd be back in the shower, locked away and confined to a small space, doing the same thing all over again. She was so tired, so drained, and so broken.

Breakfast was always oats with a handful of nuts, pumpkin and sunflower seeds, and three dates, with a small bowl of fruit and two boiled eggs. Sophia had begun to love routine through Oliver's inspiration. Except, there was no fruit left in the fruit basket. She made a mental note to stop by Sainsbury's to stock up after breakfast. A bowl of oats and eggs would do her for now.

'Bread again?' Sophia heard Oliver through the voices inside her head. He'd call her out each time, smiling whilst tugging at her rolls of fat that had begun to form around her waist, making her give up bread, pizza and all of her other favourite, but unhealthy, foods that she liked. Oliver always took care of her, looking out for both her physical and mental health, telling her what to do, what to eat and how to behave. He wasn't controlling or obsessive, he just took care of her, because that's what people do when they're in love. Sophia smiled as she took out a bowl for her oats. Nice and healthy, just how Oliver taught her.

The sound of the phone ringing spilled through into the kitchen from the living room, distracting Sophia from her thoughts.

'Hi, sorry we're not here to take your call right now…' Sophia listened to the sound of her voice on the answering machine.

'But please leave a message after the beep and we'll get back to you when we can,' followed by Oliver's voice.

'Hi.' Isabella hesitated as she spoke in almost a whisper. She sounded worried. Sophia turned her ear towards the answering machine, listening as she began to prepare her breakfast. 'Can we meet? I had a call.' Isabella's voice trembled over the machine, she was nervous. Something wasn't right. Sophia continued to listen as she sprinkled seeds onto her oats whilst waiting for her two eggs to boil. 'You probably don't want to hear this over a machine, it's important. Call me,' Isabella hesitated, still holding onto the phone. Sophia made her way into the living room and onto the sofa with her bowl of oats. Isabella didn't hang up. 'Oh, I know you're not going to call me.' She seemed distressed. Sophia knew her mum, she could tell instantly whether or not there was something wrong, just by looking at her or hearing her voice. But this time it was different. This time there was something in Isabella's voice, something that made Sophia decide that she wasn't going to listen, because she wasn't going to like it. Isabella needed to stop over-thinking.

'Apparently they've received insight. They say it could be enough to open up an investigation, if the information they have is true. They'll keep me updated but that's all I know.' Crackling sounds filled the room as she sighed into the phone. 'It's been months. I don't know how secure this source is, I don't know what they're gripping on to, but they've got something.' She hung up, refusing to break down over the phone.

Sophia sat on the sofa, glaring at the TV screen. Rachel and Chandler had been eating cheesecake off the floor in the hallway. *Friends* was on the TV but Sophia's mind was elsewhere. She tried to block it out but her head began to fill with smoke, choking any positive thought that was inside. She was cold, numb, unsure of what she was hearing, wondering whether her imagination was playing tricks on her. The sound of Isabella's voice gnawed away inside her brain, taking away her ability to think or understand what it was that Isabella was saying. An investigation? After all this time? Sophia shook her head, deciding it wasn't real. She lifted a spoonful of oats, letting *Friends* keep her company as she ate.

It wasn't easy for her to laugh and smile the way she used to. Her nightmares had begun to take over her life and everything in her world started becoming dark. Everything she said or did seemed wrong and she'd question her own choices and thoughts. Her lack of sleep and paranoia constantly left her on edge, leaving her unable to distinguish the difference between what's real and what's not. If anything could bring out even a small smile in her, it was *Friends*.

'I don't care for those kinds of programmes Soph, they're just pointless and so childish.' Oliver had said when she first introduced it to him. They'd finally gotten around to buying a TV after three months of moving in together in their new home, and it was one of the first programmes they watched together. It didn't take long for Oliver to get into it himself, but he never took back his words. Apologising and admitting he was wrong didn't come with his otherwise beautiful nature.

Neither of them followed TV programmes, other than *Friends*. They preferred watching films, and gardening, going on long walks, seeing friends and family, learning about different people, places, and culture. They'd take time out to do their own things too. Sophia would read books and paint pictures whilst Oliver would go out for his long morning strolls and work on writing his own book on self-realisation and improvement. Despite spending many hours of their days apart, they'd promised that they would take time out every Sunday, catching up on learning more about each other's personal projects, sitting together on the sofa, eating fruit and watching a few films back to back until one of them would fall asleep. It was one promise they had stuck to.

A few episodes of *Friends*, a bowl of oats and two boiled eggs later, Sophia turned off the TV. She sat there in silence on the sofa feeling refreshed as she glared at her reflection on the blank TV screen. She looked alive, free and fearless – Sophia, the lion. She continued to study herself through the screen. Her face was calm and relaxed now and radiated a glow of golden light. Her body sat tall and proud. She was in her element, in her home, safe. She sat there, imagining being surrounded by a pack of lions as they lay beside her on the grass, peacefully looking out into the horizon as the sun beamed down on them. Individually they were strong, together, they were solid.

A loud noise from the hallway interrupted her daydream, taking away the peace that surrounded her, reconnecting her back to reality. She froze. Her eyes became larger as the tiny hairs on her skin shot up instantly. She stay still, trying to listen out for footsteps or breathing or any other noise that could tell her that someone was inside the house. Oliver would usually go straight to Church on his way back from his long walk so it definitely wasn't him. She continued to listen out for signs to prove to herself that she wasn't going crazy, that she wasn't alone. But she heard nothing.

Sophia looked at her reflection on the TV screen as she stood from the sofa. The pack of lions had vanished but one animal sat there, looking back at her. It was small, skinny and frail, looking lost and scared as it stood on two legs with its two little arms just hanging to the front – a meerkat. She was certain she'd heard something in the hallway and she was certain someone was there, waiting for her. But then she wasn't sure. She was stuck in her own psychosis, unsure of what was real and what was made up. She moved quietly from the sofa and began to walk slowly towards the door.

'Run away.' 'Hide.' 'You're not safe.' The voices inside her head began to hiss at her as she moved towards danger. 'What are you doing?' 'Stop!' 'You're dead, Sophia. Dead.' The voices moved in like snakes, wrapping their words around her insides, squeezing, threatening to crush her organs as they prepared to strike her with venom, waiting for the right moment to paralyse her before swallowing her alive. She stood at the doorway and hid behind the wall as she attempted to calm her heartbeat while it slammed against the thick, dry, scaly, skin of the snakes. Her heartbeat became heavier, louder. She couldn't let it give her away. She had to make it stop. She had to make it stop but the monstrous beasts continued to slither around her insides, entwining their bodies, occasionally sticking out their tongues to taste her blood. She held her breath, a desperate attempt to slow down her heartbeat, a desperate attempt to get away. One second. Two seconds. Three. Four. Five. Six. Seven seconds. Suicide. She crashed into the doorframe, gasping for air.

'Shit!' She'd given herself away and now he knew she was there, alone, afraid, standing there on the other side of the wall. She'd given herself away. Her heart began to thump louder and even faster, slamming against its cage with each beat. She had nowhere to run. Her only way out was through the hallway, but he was there. She grabbed on to the frame of the door, holding on, tight, trembling as she forced herself to catch her breath, panting quietly. She wasn't ready to be caught, but she had nowhere to hide. Sophia held her body up against the wall, breathing deeply. She began to peer around the corner, slowly, wary. She looked for movement in the shadows. Nothing. Everything was still. Sophia had to move closer, she had to go deeper into the hallway. Whether it was to get out, or to confirm his presence in her home, she wasn't sure. Was this a trap? She couldn't tell. Her body stiffened and her hands clenched tightly into a fist as she moved through the doorway and into the hallway. No-one was there. She stood there, surveying the area in front of her, above her, behind her. She stood there, now unsure of whether or not she'd heard a noise in the first place. She wondered if it was her brain playing on the strings of her deepest fears, making her dance to the tunes that she wasn't allowed to hear. She wondered if it was her, who had tailor-made her own nightmare and bought it into reality herself. She stood there, in silence, unsure of anything.

Something on the floor caught Sophia's eye. She turned to look down at the welcome mat, at the post that lay on top of it.

'I am not crazy. There's no-one here.' She sighed. But she wasn't relieved. Post didn't arrive on Sundays. It was time to get out.

Sophia began to put on her boots as she continued to let her devious and deceitful thoughts overcome her, doubting herself, her gut and the voices inside her head. Maybe the voices had been over-reacting. Maybe it was exactly just that - all in her head. Maybe she was crazy after all.

She zipped up her black, knee-high boots. It was time to get out and stock up on groceries for the evening. She tiptoed to reach for her coat from the coat rack, slipping it on as she stood there, staring at the keys to Oliver's navy blue Audi that hung on the key holder beside the front door. All the reasons not to drive came flooding in and Sophia could feel uninvited panic walk into her body as her stomach began to tie itself up in a tight knot. Sainsbury's was only a fifteen minute drive away but Sophia was hesitant at the thought of driving alone. The taste of fear began to form in her mouth, salty and tainted. Her hands clammed up with sweat as she began to construct scenarios inside her head.

Scenario a) Oliver walks through the door. He's in a good mood. It's okay if there's no fruit, they can still watch a film together.

Scenario b) Oliver walks through the door. He's in a good mood. It's okay if there's no fruit, there's always tomorrow.

Scenario c) Oliver walks through the door. He ignores Sophia and makes his way up the stairs.

Sophia closed her eyes in disappointment. She knew what she had to do. She grabbed the keys as the cold metal sent a shiver up her arm. A warning? She didn't care. Oliver's needs and happiness came before her own. That was love. Facing your fears and being strong, doing things outside your comfort zone to make someone else happy. That was love. Oliver had told her so. She left the house.

Sophia stood outside the car, hesitant but certain about driving. Movement from inside the car caught her attention. A woman was sitting in the driver's seat. The woman looked tired and old. Her hair was thin and frail, and her eyes red and small. She glared back at Sophia. Sophia's eyes widened as fear began to stab her in her gut like a knife, slowly being inserted and twisted inside her. The voices inside her head began to scream.

'You did this.' 'Red flags.' 'You knew.'

She closed her eyes, taking herself far away, dropping the weight of her thoughts to the ground, releasing the voices inside her head, tapping out of reality, out of her thoughts, placing herself at the park, laying on the grass, as she watched the sunset beside her dad. She counted to five before opening her eyes. The woman was still there, looking back at her. Sophia was staring at her own reflection through the car window. She wondered whether she was going crazy as she stood there, confused.

'You don't know what you can do until you actually try doing it.' One of the nicer voices inside her head spoke to her. It was Oliver, the first time they sat together in the car before setting off on a long drive, with Sophia in the driver's seat. Sophia pressed the button on the key and the car doors unlocked.

It was nearly 1:30 p.m. when she pulled up into the Sainsbury's car park. The car park was packed and it had taken her just over five minutes before she found a space, at the far end, away from the entrance to the supermarket. Sophia stepped out of the car and looked around, inspecting her surroundings, preparing herself to be stuck within crowds of judgemental, snobby beasts, who'd look through her like she didn't exist. She locked the door and began walking through the car park towards the supermarket.

The sun was shining and the birds had been gliding across the skies above her, to and from the roof-tops of other stores within the retail park. Sophia walked along the car park, in and out of shadows, feeling the suns warmth one minute, and the bitterness in the air the next. The voices inside her head had begun to fall asleep through the steady sounds of traffic in the background as she approached the supermarket.

'Break!' 'Stop!' They were taken out of their trance. The voices jolted, screaming without warning as she entered Sainsbury's. The beeping sounds from the scanning machines at the checkouts filled her ears, stinging her soul as if she'd been bitten by the deadly snakes inside her. Her ears continued to ring and her heartbeat elevated. Her organs began to contract and she felt herself struggling to breathe. She wanted to go home. It wasn't real. She had to calm down and stop over-reacting. She stopped beside a stack of baskets, and reached inside her bag. She took out her headphones and connected it to her phone, drowning out the beeping of the scanners, the footsteps and murmurs of shoppers, and the voices inside her head. She picked up a basket as the sound of a flute played peacefully through her ears, putting the voices inside her head to peace. Another temporary escape. She walked, further into the supermarket, hearing the sound of her elevated breathing and heartbeat inside her ears, remembering why she never liked wearing headphones. But it was only temporary. She walked the long way around to the fruit section, scurrying around the crowd of busy shoppers, avoiding eye contact or any interaction with as many people as possible. She walked towards the shelves where the packed fruits were kept and picked out a small pack of strawberries and blueberries as well as two large papayas. She went around to the other side of the shelving unit where the bananas were and picked out a small bunch. Just in front of the bananas lived the apples, pears and her favourite, kiwis. She stopped at the crate of kiwis and put four of them in a clear, plastic bag and into her basket.

'Did you know kiwis help you sleep?' Oliver had told her once during their Sunday fruit and film night. She took them out of her basket and placed them back into the crate. She did not want to sleep. She saw a box of large watermelons piled up beside the kiwis. 'Watermelons make me smile, because look, they look like big smiles,' Oliver had once said to her as he held a piece up to his mouth. She smiled herself and picked one up, placing it into her basket. As strange as he seemed sometimes, she saw so much innocence and cuteness within him.

Sophia smiled as she continued to walk around the supermarket, still slightly on edge and paranoid as she passed through the crowds of people. A loud bang from someone's trolley as it crashed into another startled her as the sound of the flute faded from her ears. She felt the prickles of needles and glass stab at her face as her heartbeat stumbled over its own rhythm. Her head began to pound, awakening the angry voices inside her. She put her hand over her mouth to suffocate the scream that had been fermenting within. It was best she left the supermarket.

Sophia dropped her basket, turning away to leave but scenario C stopped her. She imagined Oliver coming home, ignoring her as if she didn't exist. She sunk a little as her insides began to feel as though they were being shredded at the thought of being ignored by the person she loved. She picked up her basket and went to stand in the queue, nervously.

Finally, she left the store and made her way through the car park. It was dark and thick, grey clouds blanketed the sky. The birds had disappeared and the air felt dead, giving off a warning that, at any moment, the heavens would open, blessing the car park and everyone within it, with rain. Sophia held on to her shopping bags tightly as she walked towards her car. She scurried, trying to avoid being caught in the showers that were on its way. She looked up at the dark clouds directly above her, walking faster towards the car but it was too late. Sophia felt a heavy splash of rain drop onto her head, followed by another not too long after.

'Oh God, not yet!' she whispered under her breath as she sped up towards the car with her head down almost as though she was hiding. She glanced up quickly as she began to cross over to the other side of the car park. Thick drops of rain started to disperse from the sky. The headlights from the other cars blurred her vision but she continued to walk towards the car, looking up now and again to avoid coming in the way of other people or vehicles.

She stopped. The rain began to fall heavily but Sophia didn't care. Her eyes were glued to a figure in the distance, standing by the passenger side of her car, his eyes stared right back at her. He was wearing muddy blue jeans and an unzipped, dark brown bomber jacket over a navy blue hoodie. His hood was up, head down, eyes on her. The man from the park. Her body filled with fear, with anger, sadness and every other non-pleasant emotion that she'd washed away in the shower earlier that morning. Her shoulders tensed up and her grip onto her shopping bags tightened. She turned around instantly as she headed towards the supermarket, scurrying fast, like a meerkat.

'Don't cry, don't panic, this isn't real, none of it is real.' She tried to assure herself. The rain continued to fall down heavily and her sight began to blur even more as her eyes drowned in water. The shadows and reflections created by the bright headlights of other cars stretched across the car park. The shadows, the darkness, and this man watching her from beside her car put Sophia back in her cage, trapped with the voices inside her head.

She scurried, trying to get back into the

supermarket to be with the crowd of people she had been avoiding not too long ago. She scurried back to safety. But she was still afraid. Afraid not only of this strange man who had been stalking her in reality, not only of the nightmares that she'd been running from for over seven months, but of herself, her reactions, her behaviour, and her inability to handle any negative situation in the right way. She was terrified.

After spending thirty minutes walking around Sainsbury's, waiting for the rain to stop and for the strange man to disappear, Sophia finally made it home. She was safe.

She sat, curled up on the living room sofa underneath a thick, grey blanket with her hands wrapped around a mug of green tea. The TV was on and despite her eyes being fixated on the screen, her thoughts were running wild, taking her back to the past.

A line about fear and dreams from *The Lord of the Flies* took over her mind out of nowhere. She was told by one of the characters in the book, that fear and dreams couldn't hurt her. But that wasn't true. She was confused. Fear did hurt, just as much as a dream. The voices inside her head told her the same. The book lied to her, betrayed her. Sophia didn't know who to trust or what to believe. She moved the blanket off of her and placed the mug on top of a small table on the side of the sofa. She stood up and made her way into the kitchen, still afraid, confused. Sophia's nightmares and reality were slowly becoming one. Staying awake to avoid dreaming was one thing, but this man was real now, and her fear only became stronger. If dreams couldn't hurt her, reality definitely could. It was driving her insane.

She stood in the kitchen as she filled the kettle before ripping a banana away from its bunch. She began to peel it, still thinking, still trying to work out the truth from her nightmares and reality. The phone rang. She bit into the banana whilst opening the door to one of the kitchen cabinets and took out a mug.

'Hi, sorry we're not here to take your call right now…' Sophia listened to the sound of her voice on the answering machine as she took another bite of her banana.

'But please leave a message after the beep and we'll get back to you when we can,' followed by Oliver's voice.

By now, the water had boiled. Sophia stuck a green tea bag in her mug and poured water over it, forgetting about the full mug of green tea that she was holding on to not too long ago. She took another bite from her banana as she listened to the voicemail.

'Hi, it's me again,' Sophia's heart filled with dread as the voice from the answering machine exposed even more hurt, hesitation and discomfort than it did before. 'I'm worried about you. You don't get back to my calls, you don't answer your door, you're avoiding everyone who tries to help.' It was Isabella. Sophia continued to eat her banana. 'I know, it's not easy and it probably never will be, but have faith and don't ever lose hope, no matter how hard life gets, if it's not alright in the end, it's simply not the end. You told me that remember? Call me when you're ready. I know my message before would have come as a shock. I'm sorry. I'm here if you need to talk.' Isabella hung up.

Sophia took another bite from her banana and rolled her eyes. It wasn't real. She picked up her new mug of green tea and walked to the bin. She pushed her foot down on the paddle and the lid shot up. She looked into the bin before disposing her banana skin, staring and frowning in disappointment after identifying two empty cans of Budweiser buried inside the black bag. Had Oliver taken up drinking? She wasn't sure. She ignored it and headed out of the kitchen and back onto the living room sofa.

She sat there, as Isabella's words repeated over and over through her ears. Sophia never understood why Isabella was so worried all the time. As much as Sophia loved her mum, Isabella was an over-thinker and became easily troubled over everything. Nothing was going to happen. Sophia had Oliver, and he was the kindest and most genuine human being on earth.

Sophia stared at the TV, but she wasn't watching.

CHAPTER FIVE

Sophia didn't understand why Isabella worried about them so much. Isabella had known Oliver since he was thirteen, and out of all of Sophia's friends, Isabella had been closest to Oliver the most. She didn't need to worry.

Isabella had first met Sophia's new friends at a barbeque that she had organised in the summer after they settled into their new home. Sophia had known Lucy, Oliver and Tristan for around six months before meeting Isabella. Isabella held a barbeque at her home, inviting their new neighbours, Sophia's friends, and a few of her own friends from work. She found the whole situation daunting, being shy herself and having never hosted such an event before, but she felt as though she needed to do it for Sophia's sake after making her leave behind all of her memories and the friends she had known throughout her entire childhood in the town she grew up in.

It was at this barbeque when Oliver saw what a mother's love was. He saw Isabella's kindness as it bounced through her smile, her eyes and in her voice.

***

The sound of meat sizzling over on the smoldering metal grills of the barbeque trickled into the air amongst the lingering smoke. The aromas teased the guests as they bathed in the vapours, intoxicated by the fragrances that oozed out of the wings and breasts. Groups of people were scattered around the small garden, talking and laughing over the sound of the radio that was playing into the garden through the kitchen window.

Lucy had introduced herself to the other guests, while Tristan had joined the neighbour in manning the barbeque. Sophia and Isabella walked around happily, welcoming guests, pouring drinks and offering snacks and making sure everyone was having a good time. Oliver was more reserved and shy and was sat hidden away in the corner, watching. He watched as Sophia and Isabella worked as a team, preparing the food for the barbeque, the snacks, the drinks, going around speaking to everyone. He watched Isabella run the palm of her hand across Sophia's cheek, smiling. He watched as she lovingly tucked strands of Sophia's hair away from her face and behind her ear. He watched, innocently, in envy.

The more he saw, the more he began to resent his own mum. He was happy for Sophia, but he wanted what she had.

Seeing how Isabella and Sophia were with each other ignited a fire inside him that burned though his skin, turning his insides into ash. It reminded him of his own childhood, the lack of affection and his desperateness to be wanted and loved. He was desperate for a mother like Isabella who adored her child more than anything, and he despised them for rubbing it deep into his wounds. He'd only known Sophia for six months but had begun to dislike her through watching her laugh and smile with her mum in front of him. He hated her for all of the insecurities he had within himself, casting himself as a victim, refusing to swallow even an ounce of his own truth. He watched them, and imagined how his life would have been had he been given the right family. The right mother. One like Isabella. He fantasised about how his life would be with Isabella for a mum, true happiness and real love, where he wouldn't need to hurt.

From that day, Oliver had made a decision. He knew what life he wanted, and he was going to get it, providing he had the perfect strategy in place.

***

Oliver had gotten over his issues at the barbeque during the summer break. He'd forgiven Sophia and

Isabella for their actions, understanding that they were unaware of his past. In fact, he had become fonder of Sophia. He spent more time at her house, sometimes Tristan and Lucy joined him, and other times he'd go on his own. He helped Sophia and Isabella with bits around the house, making him feel better about himself after having had set the devil free on his previous thoughts towards them. Isabella loved him and over time, had developed her own connection with him, like the bond between a mother and her son, just like he'd prayed for.

Isabella loved and treated all of Sophia's friends like her own, sharing the love equally between them. Tristan would visit Isabella now and again on the weekends, to accompany her over coffee and homemade biscuits. She loved them and loved how they all looked out for her daughter, for her, and for each other. Oliver would spend more and more time with Sophia and Isabella and soon enough, he had become a part of the furniture. He would talk to Isabella about his issues and home life and was able to confide in her and trust her, listening to her advice and stories of both her own previous experiences and Sophia's too. She instantly took him under her wing and he began to see her like she was his own mum.

Over time, he was able to open up to Isabella more, and would tell her things about his childhood, sharing some of his thoughts that he'd never shared with anyone. He told her how his dad was an alcoholic and gambled his way through life to feed his constant desire for the taste of beer, not once thinking about the effects it would have on his family. He told her how ever since he could remember, his dad had always smelt like beer and sweat, always slurring, walking through the front door in the early hours of the morning, stumbling into the house, sometimes grumbling, sometimes shouting, ignoring the pain he was putting his wife and son through. He told her how he despised his mum for never doing anything about it, and for falling pregnant with him in the first place knowing too well what kind of life she was going to bring her son into. He told her how he was never comforted the way a child needed to be comforted growing up, how his mum was always busy working, too focused on earning money to pay bills and put food on the table, and how, throughout all of Oliver's life, how he was made to feel like an inconvenience.

He told Isabella everything. How unlike other children who aspired to be like at least one of their parents, he didn't want to be anything like his. How he didn't want them in his life, how they didn't deserve to be happy. He had even admitted to having thoughts about hurting them, how at night he'd lay in bed, wondering whether or not to walk into their bedroom, and take them away from any punishment they were to face in the name of karma. Saving them, setting them free, despite what they did to him. He told her how he'd been through so much hurt and depression during his childhood, how he had no-one who cared enough to help, and how he had even attempted to end his life on a few occasions.

Isabella was concerned, seeing the look in his eyes as they glazed over with a dark shadow of nastiness. She was worried, more for the wellbeing of his friend, her daughter. She was alarmed and ready to raise her concerns to Sophia until he told her about his illness and how it had changed him.

He told her of his cancer and how it had saved him. How he had changed his lifestyle after overcoming chemotherapy and surgery. He told her how he'd begun to remove any negativity from around him because of it. How having the brain tumour saved him, making him open his eyes to a second chance at life. He told her how he needed to walk away from the things that put him down. How he was going to cling onto those that made him feel good instead. How he planned to work when he was able, save up and leave his parents to be closer to his newly found mum. He told her how cancer had changed him, making him appreciate life, making him realise that he didn't want to die. He told her about all the many patients he'd met, who were going through chemotherapy, how he'd listen to their positivity and strength to fight and the stories they'd tell. How it all made him see how much more there was to life outside the four walls of his bedroom – the bigger picture. He told her how he had reincarnated into someone else, someone who wanted to change the lives of so many people by focusing on positivity and self-realisation, to become the one thing in life that everyone wants to be – happy. And he did just that. Being with Sophia made her the happiest she had ever been, and Isabella recognised that, despite there being something about Oliver that didn't quite fit.

It was during the last few days of sixth form and Oliver had turned up at their home one afternoon. Sophia had been off sick for a few days with the flu and Oliver decided to check up on his friend after his classes were over. He was always welcome in Isabella's home, so much that he was comfortable enough to treat it like his own, and both Isabella and Sophia loved that. Isabella was out at a work Christmas dinner, and Oliver was adamant to stay with Sophia until Isabella reached home. She and Oliver had talked for hours. Late afternoon had turned into evening and evening to night, until the early hours of the morning. They bounced from one subject to the next, laughing and joking around, playing 'what if' scenarios, teasing each other and talking about life. Neither of them wanted the conversations to end. Sophia saw something in Oliver that she'd failed to see before. He made her feel so comfortable around him, and around herself. Even if she tried to run, it was too late. There was a force or some kind of energy between them and both of them could feel it, despite something inside her, reminding her that this was never part of her plan.

Isabella too had noticed how well the two of them got along. She had come home late in the evening, and sat with them for a few moments, snacking on fruit and sipping camomile tea before heading off to bed. Isabella could sense something, and felt the aura of joy and true happiness coming from within Sophia as she and Oliver talked. Sophia saw the same in Isabella as she watched her eyes glisten with the same happiness at the thought of her daughter being happy. It had been a long time for both of them, and they owed it to Oliver for being the one to make them feel good.

That one evening, at the dining table in Isabella's kitchen, was the beginning of a different life for all of them. For the first time since her dads passing, Oliver had made Sophia smile from deep within. It wasn't a pretend one, it was real. Isabella saw how much happiness this troubled, yet innocent boy bought to her daughter's life, and promised herself that she would stick by him and be the mother that he needed her to be, for the sake of her daughter's happiness. And in return, Oliver gave his love to Sophia.

Oliver was different compared to anyone Sophia had ever met. He was a gentleman, despite having never opened a door for Sophia, or for any other woman. He didn't believe it was those traits that made a man a gentleman. The traits of opening a door or pulling out a chair for a woman just for being a woman didn't fit his perception of what a real gentleman was, and so it was wrong. Sophia respected his beliefs and didn't expect him to take those gestures upon him to prove his feelings towards her, especially when she was perfectly capable of opening her own doors, pulling out her own chairs and carrying her own bags. He was different, and she fell for him even more because of the things he didn't do.

In her eyes, he was sweet and charming, kind, sensitive and loveable. He was full of positive energy, determined and focused to live his life, fulfilling his goals and chasing happiness. It was the little things he did that were the big things, the game-changers. He took pride in seeing people succeed and do well with his support. Sophia loved that about him, she loved how much he tried to help people, how much he tried to understand them, and learn more about those he was close to. He wasn't out there to impress anyone, compete against anyone, or please anyone. What he did for others was genuine, he cared. He wanted to help people and never asked for anything in return. It made him feel good.

But it was the smallest of things he did that made her fall for him. He'd pay attention to her in ways that nobody else ever did. He'd learn her likes and dislikes, remember the type of coffee she drank, her favourite pizza toppings, her favourite film, song, everything, without ever asking. He would take time to understand her as a person, through listening to her words and observing her reactions, enough to be able to tell when she was feeling down, when she wanted to be alone and when she needed someone around. He'd pay genuine interest in the person she was beneath what she portrayed, and taught her what she

79

needed to do to improve herself, to be a better person, like him. Sometimes she was creeped out by how much he knew and how much information he had taken in about her, and sometimes his actions would send red signals to her gut, making her feel wary. The voices inside her head would tell her to be cautious, telling her it was too good to be true, that there was something about him. And there *was* something about him, something so sweet and kind. He gave her so much. He would fill her with positivity and the ability to do things she never thought possible. He made her feel confident in herself and she'd feel so good, that she was able to ignore her gut feelings, placing the cause of her mixed emotions on her own troubled, childhood experiences.

Weeks turned into months and months to years, and Sophia and Oliver had grown together. Ever since Sophia had known Oliver, he had encouraged and pushed her to follow her dreams. His calm approach to life, his mannerisms and everything else about him made him so much more desirable to her over the years, and as Sophia spent more and more time with him, he became that much more irresistible. She aspired to be like him and fell madly in love with him, going against everything she believed in as a child, about love and relationships. But it was fine, because they were soulmates. Sophia would support Oliver and he'd do the same in return, protecting her against any harm. Oliver had experienced and witnessed too much nastiness whilst growing up and once he realised he had the power to make his own decisions and rule his own life, he held on to it, for himself and for Sophia, who had neither the power nor the strength. Sophia recognised the innocence of his intentions no matter how many times they made her bleed. She'd fallen for him, blinded by the light that he'd shone in her eyes. Blinded by the warm sensation of love inside her that was stronger than any other feeling she'd ever experienced. Stronger than the times when he would pierce her soul with insecurities and paranoia, when he would lock her in the dark and make her feel like she was unworthy. Unworthy of light, unworthy of him. But he loved her too, and so she would bury those bad feelings deep within her, excusing him each time. He only wanted her love, and she hadn't shown it well enough. It was her own fault and so her punishments were lessons. Everything he did, he did for her own good, and he would always make that clear, reassuring Sophia that it was all because he loved her and wanted her to be strong and happy. And she would believe it.

Sophia sat on the sofa staring at the images on the TV screen. She sat there, letting her memories of Oliver fill her soul as she waited for him to come home from the church. She sat there and smiled. Isabella did not need to worry. Sophia had Oliver.

CHAPTER SIX

The evening had finally arrived. Sophia closed the curtains of the living room to block out the nasty weather framed by the windowpane. It was dark and wet and although the street was empty, it was filled with the shadows and reflections of trees, lampposts and parked cars along the street. Inside, the atmosphere was quite the opposite. Golden light was sprinkled across the room like fairy dust, creating a soft glow around everything it touched. The warmth of the fireplace and the sound of the wood burning as the flames danced in the middle of the fireplace bought magic into the room. It was airy and peaceful, just the perfect setting for a nice Sunday night in for two.

A mug of green tea and a large bowl of sliced watermelon, mango and papaya sat on the small table by the sofa, ready to be consumed during Sophia and

Oliver's Sunday night film. They snuggled on the sofa together, underneath the warm and fluffy, grey blanket. Oliver sat at the end, within easy reach of the fruit bowl and green tea. His feet were up on the little coffee table which sat between the sofa and the TV. Sophia lay next to him with both her legs folded beside her as she leaned into Oliver, placing her head gently on his shoulder. Both her arms were wrapped around one of his as he rested it on his leg. His other arm hung from the arm of the sofa with his fingers slowly caressing the rim of the mug on the table, as the opening credits of the film filled the TV screen.

First up, was *Stand By Me,* released in 1986 and one of Sophia's favourite films of all time. Sophia smiled. She was content. She was in her safe place, watching one of her favourite films with her favourite human being. That moment and everything within it, was perfect. Sophia felt herself sink further into Oliver's shoulder as he pushed himself into the sofa, breathing deeply. The film started. Sophia kissed Oliver's arm and squeezed it tight.

It was only a few minutes into the film when the sound of the house phone ringing filled the room. Sophia and Oliver kept their eyes on the TV screen as the phone continued to ring. It was their Sunday film night and their time together. Neither of them flinched. They stared at the screen, blocking out the ringing as if it wasn't there. The call went to voicemail.

'Hi, sorry we're not here to take your call right

now…' Sophia's voice chirped, happily on the answering machine.

'But please leave a message after the beep and we'll get back to you when we can,' Oliver's voice followed.

'Hey. T here.' Tristan's voice was muffled as he shouted over the sound of traffic in the background. 'Dropped by earlier, as you probably know, just checking in, again.' He sounded tired and out of breath as if he was walking back home from his evening run. 'Had some guy come down earlier, some investigator or something, asking all sorts of questions. On a Sunday as well.' He paused for a moment before continuing. 'Weird. It's been what, seven months? Call me when you can. Peace out.' He hung up the phone.

Sophia and Oliver ignored the message as if they couldn't hear it and continued to immerse themselves into the film. Oliver reached for the fruit bowl picking first at the watermelon. Sophia smiled as she pulled the fluffy blanket closer to her body, tucking it in tightly beneath her chin and around her legs. She stared at his reflection on the TV. He was sweating nervously as he also stared into his own eyes through the screen. Neither of them had been watching the film. They'd both heard Tristan's message.

Nearly thirty minutes had passed. The bowl of fruit was empty. The room became darker, but was still lit dimly by a slight glow from the fire which had begun to die out. Warmth filled the room and the continuous sound of wood burning made Sophia feel more and more relaxed. Her eyes began to get heavy and body limp as she found herself falling into a deep, deep sleep.

***

Sophia had been running within the darkness of the night for nearly two hours, amongst the shadows of the trees. Dead leaves crackled from beneath her feet and sweat dripped from her face as she continued to run, looking for a way to escape from this man with the blurred face. Blotches of dirt covered her nose and cheeks after being forced to the ground by the slippery surface of the park. Her clothes were torn by the twigs and nettles as they attempted to slow her down further. The moonlight was hidden above a canopy of branches, leaving her with only enough light to witness the darkness. Nature had turned on her.

The park was misty and eerie and the air was ice cold. The streams of moonlight that were denied access to pass through the trees, cast long, dark shadows of every branch from every tree across the ground and onto the path. Sophia ran in and out of the shadows. The sound of her heartbeat pulsating through her body surrendered to the silence as she tried to escape. The exit to the park had disappeared. Sophia knew was trapped.

She stopped and stood still, looking around her,

for a sign, an exit, for something. Nothing. She stood in the darkness of the shadows, afraid. Fog filled her head as a sudden chill of fear ran down her spine. It was the same fear that she felt when she learned of her dad's death, of his murder. She bit her lip, so hard that she could taste her sweet blood as it escaped onto her tongue, oozing out from her cracked lips in thick, little droplets.

The sound of her heartbeat became louder and heavier and the muscles inside her body became weaker. She fell to the ground, hopeless. She sat there, feeling empty like a dark void, while her soul, silenced and hollow, crept in the shadows like a ghost. Sophia's face filled with streams of tears as she cried for a way out, for strength, for all of this to end. She knew someone was watching her. She knew she needed to run. But where to? And for how long? Running away and escaping were just temporary measures. He was getting closer, smarter. She was getting tired. She felt as though her spirit was ready to part from her body, like a dislocated arm, pulled from its socket. Temporarily. Except death was permanent. She sat there, fighting the urge to lie down, fighting the urge to sleep, unable to think, fatigued, limp like wet laundry hanging on a washing line on a cold day.

The fog inside her head began to retreat as she sat on the floor in silence, struck by the realisation that she was not going to win this ugly game that she was being forced to play. A sudden sound of rustling escaped into the air around her as she watched the leaves glide gently across the park. The branches swayed slightly as the gentle sounds of the rustling and crunching leaves continued to play like instruments, softly in her ears. She focused on the sounds of the lullaby as they played peacefully, making her feel calm and content. But nature was teasing her, lying to her, pretending like it was all okay, like a sad clown with a painted smile. The warm but vicious and creepy kind of smile, forced and disturbing, bringing out the devil through its eyes, transforming peace into screams of pain. The harmonic melodies began to change as they scraped through her ears like nails to a chalk board. It wasn't the midnight breeze that she could hear. There was no draught around her, and there was no wind to cause the leaves to rustle. The noise was coming from one place. Above her. Someone was there, but she couldn't see.

The banging of her heartbeat, the shrieks of her cries and the voices inside her head ceased to exist as silence struck her body. She sat there, with her head up, searching for a reason to be as scared as she was, looking for a threat, wondering whether it was her mind attacking her, punishing her. Self-harm like deep cuts to her wrists, invisible when on the inside. She was scarred by the fear in her imagination. It was the fear inside her, spreading like a virus that existed only in her mind, like a kind of madness, only she wasn't mad. But it was making her ill.

She looked around like a meerkat on duty, with her

energy focusing only on the stillness around her. Everything had turned silent. Sophia began to look around, staring deeply into the trees ahead of her, above her. There was nothing there. She continued to survey the area, looking for any movement from within the trees, but they refused to reveal anything.

Darkness trickled among her as she continued to remain still in the avoidance of challenging the demons around her. She closed her eyes as an attempt to switch her focus to sound, listening out for any kind of noise. Nothing but the sound of her own heart thudding heavily against her chest filled her ears like a ticking bomb ready to explode. This man was smart.

Sophia was tired as she sat there listening out for nothing, knowing he was playing, teasing, trying to take control over her. A few minutes had passed. Sophia sat there in the middle of the park, eyes closed and heartbeat now slowed. A sense of tranquillity filled her body as she calmed herself down, breathing deeply, lying to herself, pretending that it was all okay. She began to enter into a state of meditation, ignoring her surroundings, running away inside her mind. Sweet humming left her mouth as the gentle pitched notes to the soundtrack of *Stand By Me* filled the silence. She held her arms around her, cradling herself as she rocked herself back and forth, trying to maintain her sense of peace and comfort. Her body became heavy as she moved further towards the ground, preparing herself to go into deep sleep.

'No,' Sophia awakened the voices inside her head. 'Don't do it.' 'Not again.' The voices refused to let her sleep on the park floor, exposed, weak and vulnerable to this man with the blurred face. He was watching her and she knew it. She couldn't see him, she couldn't hear him, but he was there. She could feel him.

She opened her eyes. Everything now seemed so much darker than before. She looked around her, deep into the trees ahead of her and still, no sign of anyone or anything. She continued to stare into the branches. There was definitely someone there, watching her, she knew it, she was certain. Silence and emptiness surrounded her but she wasn't alone, the voices inside her head told her so.

Sophia was confused, wondering what the man with the blurred face was waiting for. She was right there, exposed and defenseless. With no other option and no way out, she lay on the ground and closed her eyes as she began to wait. But almost instantly, the trees began to shake uncontrollably. Sophia opened her eyes as they filled with horror and shock. The trees were moving, creating shadows that formed silhouettes of people through the branches. The shadows were stretched above her, looking down on her. Her vision became blurred as tears filled her eyes but she knew she wasn't seeing things. This was real. It was a nightmare, but it was real. Sophia was certain. The sound of her heartbeat began to take over as she felt herself getting into a state of panic. She was kidnapped, held hostage in her own nightmare, being tortured by her own mind. But she wasn't going crazy. This was real. She felt vomit rise in her throat as her pupils dilated. Her brain fired up like a match to a box of fireworks. She felt the fear building in the pit of her stomach. Not the fear of being caught, not the fear of being trapped inside her own mind, or being left in the darkness, alone, but the fear of facing the truth, and accepting it. It burned her soul.

She closed her eyes, attempting to run away, telling herself that she was somewhere else, at home, with Oliver. She was desperate to escape. But the rustling of the leaves and branches wouldn't let her leave. Sweat blanketed her body and the fireworks in her brain were ready to explode.

Silence. Everything stood still. The sound of her heart thumping rapidly against her chest became obsolete, the voices inside her head suffocated by the blood that spilled from her inner scars, the sound of her breath as she gasped for air, muted. Sophia opened her eyes. She had no choice.

The trees had vanished. Sophia lay there, on the park floor, glaring at the shadows that the trees had left behind. She moved to sit herself up as she began to take in her new surroundings. Her eyes were drawn to the blackness as she followed them from the roots all the way up. Her heart stopped and the voices began to scream inside her head as she jolted back, terrified with what she was seeing above her. The tall and stretched shadows had formed darker shadows within them and the silhouettes began to look like faces. Faces of those she knew, of those who she was close to. She saw Oliver, Isabella, her dad, Tristan, and Lucy in each of the shadows. Each of them looking horrified and scared as though they'd seen something devastating that Sophia was yet to see. Sophia continued to stare into the shadowed faces, trying to understand what it was they were attempting to tell her. Another sign? She didn't understand. Could this have been a message from the man with the blurred face? She closed her eyes, trying to run away once again from what she was seeing. But the faces were already embedded onto the insides of her eyelids. She had no choice but to keep looking into each face as they each glared right back at her. She'd seen fear many times before, and this was no illusion. This was real.

Sophia began to panic as her heart thumped even faster, drowning out the silence as the thudding began to get louder. She tried taking deep breaths, eyes still closed, but the faces were still there, watching her, tormenting her.

'What have I done?' she cried out but no one answered.

The sound of water crashing against the pond in the distance filled her ears. She turned her head towards the sound. Nothing. Someone had turned it on. She wasn't paranoid. She was certain she wasn't alone. This was real. Someone was there.

Sophia's stance didn't change. She sat there

looking up but listening to the sounds of the water as it began to get louder and louder, drowning out her recent torturing of the display of distraught faces of everyone she loved.

She sat there, hopeless on the park floor, in the open space, still exposed to the shadows and the darkness. She sat there, exhibiting her pain and fear, and her loss of will to carry on running. She wanted for someone or something to see her, to take her, to help her, whichever was easier that would put an end to it all. But no-one came. He was teasing her. It wasn't time for her to give up, she didn't want to either, but she was tired.

Sophia closed her eyes and began to pray as tears rolled down her delicate and pale face. It was her last attempt at getting through whatever this was. She prayed, not knowing if it was the right thing to do for a non-believer, but there was something about bad situations that bought people close to Him. She prayed for daylight, for the strength to get away. Hope and faith were the only things that were left to try to keep her going. She was desperate.

She prayed heavily with her eyes shut tight. She prayed and cried even harder upon seeing each of the expressions on the faces that she saw within the shadows of the trees, the faces that were engraved onto the insides of her eyelids. Her family. She had to save them. She had to get out. Sophia was ready. She opened her eyes, which had now become red and glazed with determination to escape. She stood up, looking around her, wanting to see this man with the blurred face, wanting for him to approach her. She was ready to make herself the heroine of her nightmare. But he didn't let her. Sophia knew he wouldn't come, not on her terms. For now, her mission had to be *escape*.

A little flash caught her eye, distracting her from her moment of power. Was God answering her prayers? The flash appeared again in the distance, beyond the darkness of the shadows as an orange light flickered from a lamppost that stood at the entrance to the park. There it was. Her escape. Sophia looked at the bench which wasn't too far from the lamppost. It disappeared and reappeared with every flicker of light. Her eyes were drawn to it like a moth to a flame. All of the signs read danger but she needed to try. The bench where the man with the blurred face originally sat, was empty. She knew this was a trap, but she also knew this could be her only chance to escape. Either that or it was God, opening the doors to the exit, letting her walk out freely. She wasn't sure.

'Stop.' 'You know, Sophia, you know.' The voices inside her head rose from the dead as they began to scream, warning her, protecting her. Sophia moved towards the gates, slowly, entranced by the light, but confused and wary of the sudden ease of escaping. This was too easy. She increased her pace, speeding up taking longer strides until she found herself to be running, fast and desperate to get away as she held on to that last bit of hope, faith and strength that she had developed inside her.

But her instincts were right. Sophia felt as though her soul had left her body, giving up as her heart began to sink, along with all of her organs as they dropped inside her. She slowed down, feeling deflated and hollow. The desperation and motivation in her eyes were replaced with emptiness and despair as she watched the path in front of her stretch longer as the shadows alongside her grew taller. She continued to move towards the gates slowly holding on to the last ounce of hope. It began to fade as she witnessed her only escape move further and further away from her. The orange light continued to flicker faster in the distance and soon enough, along with the bench and the way out, the light had disappeared. He was teasing her, holding her hostage in his vile game as he set her up for his next move, planning each of her steps in advance, playing her like a puppet on strings so she could give him the sick pleasure that he craved.

Sophia looked around. She was stuck. She was stuck in the dark, alone and exposed in the open space, with the all the shadows and faces, with her fear, and all the sadness and misery she could ever have possibly imagined. Imagined. Is that what this was? Sophia was confused. No. This was real.

Every bit of hope and energy she had inside her was lost. The sound of her inner voice reassuring her that she would get away was no longer there, the ounce of courage to run, gone. The newly found faith that God would lead her out, vanished. Loneliness crept up on her, but still, she knew she wasn't alone. She was never alone.

She stood there, looking around, examining the shadows of trees that weren't there, then at the area of nothingness where the exit to the park was not so long ago. She froze. Cold air wrapped around her as she stood in disbelief, confused and numb. She stared into the area of nothingness. The bench had appeared, far in the distance. Sophia didn't move. Around her, park benches began to appear and disappear in instant flashes. One. Two. Three. No sound other than the one of her heart pacing filled her ears. Four. Five. Sweat dripped down her face as nerves and fear swept over her body. Six. Seven. Eight benches surrounded her, enclosing her into a space with nowhere to go. She kept still, waiting, watching, numb. She jolted to the right, as she saw something move on one of the benches. A crow was sat on the corner. Its beady, dark eyes glared at Sophia. She glared back.

Out of nowhere, a flock of crows flew into the park. They were larger than usual, soaring over Sophia from all directions. She looked down at the shadows created by their long, black wings and thick, dark bodies moving quickly above her head. Sophia crouched down to the ground in a ball, covering her ears from the deafening sounds of the birds flapping their thick, heavy wings over her.

They began to disperse themselves in different

directions towards the benches. At each bench sat the silhouettes of twelve crows that had been accompanying another figure. A man. The same man that she'd been seeing everywhere. He wore muddy blue jeans and an unzipped, dark brown bomber jacket over a navy blue hoodie. He sat at each of the benches. Hood up, head down, and each of their eyes staring right at her.

Sophia's heart raced as her breath became heavier. She began to panic as she realised there really was no other way out.

***

The vulgar sound of a car horn came roaring into the room from outside, startling Sophia and awakening her from her sleep. The sound vibrated through her ears, and continued even after it had stopped. Her eyes opened wide as the sound of the horn scored through her eardrums like a devil rat gnawing through the raw, pink flesh of her ear. Her imagination and paranoia caused the sound to repeat itself over and over until she closed her eyes and put her hands over her ears. The taste of sweet blood filled her mouth as she realised she was bleeding.

Silence filled the room. Sophia opened her eyes, slowly letting in the light from the TV as she tried to make out her whereabouts. She lay on the sofa, her muscles were tensed and she was soaked in her own sweat. She observed the room blindly as her eyes adjusted to the light from the TV in front of her. She was confused.

Ben E King's *Stand By Me* soundtrack was on in the background in the closing credits of the film. She looked around, realising she was at home, safe. She sighed, and her muscles released as she immersed herself back into the sofa comfortably. She lay for a while, taking deep breaths to calm herself further from the nightmare she'd just experienced. The closing credits to the film had ended. She continued to lay there with her eyes closed, pretending to be somewhere else. She took herself to the park on a nice sunny day, as she lay beside her dad as they watched the clouds go by.

The DVD began to replay itself and the trailers of other films began to play in the background. Sophia felt a sudden breeze and opened her eyes again, coming out of her daydream. The fire had burned out and Oliver had gone.

'Great,' she whispered underneath her breath, sighing in annoyance for allowing herself to fall asleep.

Oliver would usually go to bed early without disturbing her whenever she'd fall asleep. It wasn't always she'd sleep peacefully let alone sleep at all and so he'd leave her to it whenever she did sleep.

She lay there on the sofa, still wrapped up in the fluffy, grey blanket, humming to the soundtrack of *Stand By Me*. She began to sing in what was almost a whisper as she came to terms with her nightmare. Her loneliness and lack of conversation with Oliver or anyone else made her feel weak. She was surrounded by nothing but isolation, dark figures, and the voices inside her head, and there was no-one there who was going to save her from any of it.

She continued to sing quietly to herself. She was tired, drained, ready to give up, and go away, running away once again, from reality, the facts and her true feelings.

Bobby Day's *Rockin' Robin* filled the room as *Stand By Me* began to play again on the TV screen. She tapped one foot against the other to the beat as she lay on the sofa, pretending she wasn't affected by everything that had been happening. The blanket slid down to the floor as she tapped away. A cold shiver ran through her body. Sophia sat up onto the sofa, picking up the blanket and wrapping it around her legs. The empty bowl of fruit sat on the little table beside the sofa. On the coffee table opposite her, were a bunch of pages that Oliver had been writing for his self-help book.

He was about three quarters of the way in and wasn't far off from completing the first draft. Sophia used what seemed like the last bit of energy she had in her, to reach for the pages before tucking herself back into the blanket again and re-making herself comfortable. She began to read.

There is a lot of hate, greed and pain in this world. Only man is capable of turning something so beautiful into something so ugly. Look what we have done to the world, to each other. So many people are horrible to each other and I never understood why, but over time, through experiences and obstacles and acts of others, it makes sense. I myself have made wrong choices, it still eats me up at night and I can't understand how one soul can be so unkind to another. Where does it all start? When will it end? Sometimes I wonder if I'd be better off if I wasn't in this world at all. It's not for people like me.

The Green Mile had always been a favourite of Oliver's and had inspired him to touch on the acts of man following one of the scenes from the film. Oliver had been through enough trauma throughout his lifetime where hating people and giving up seemed like the best option. There were times he would feel like no-one understood his level of sensitivity, that only he could feel pain the way he did, the pain of others as well as his own. He felt different to others, and being different meant not fitting in, not belonging It was through watching *The Green Mile*, when he realised he wasn't alone. Despite it being just a film, it was just another sign from God that told him to keep going. And so he did. Sophia continued to read.

Giving up is and has always been the easier option, but never the right one. There is always a source for an evil act, but there is not an evil person. Kindness is contagious, as are acts of evil. Sometimes, when you've been through traumatic experiences that are stronger than what your mind can handle, it becomes less difficult to go against your own values. It becomes less difficult to become just as bad as the people who have hurt you. It's all a cycle. Recognising and accepting what you have done is the first step. Moving on and doubling the kindness is the next. You can't reach everyone, but you can reach.

In times of darkness, in times of hatred and evil, where our own deepest, darkest secrets of time eat at us every single day, it is important to find the strength to overcome it, to forgive yourself and those around you, and focus on what's actually important.

Sophia put the page down. She was proud. Proud of Oliver's strength. Throughout his childhood Oliver had constantly been surrounded by negativity, hearing he won't ever be someone, or get anything good from his education. Society had wronged his parents and they had wronged society back, reaping in whatever benefit's they could get. Everything was tit for tat, and 'right now'. If he did something or wanted to do something that didn't provide instant results, then it was a waste of time. The word 'can't' repeated over and over in his head constantly until he believed it was true. He heard it every night, accepting he would never have a life like the ones of the characters he'd read about in his books, or of the people he'd watch on TV. He was forced to live in a world of darkness where he was only able to watch other people be happy.

Free, self-assigned, after school counseling sessions didn't help him either. Before he met Isabella, he was never comfortable enough to be able to tell anyone the truth about what was happening or how he was feeling. He tried to help himself, he was aware he needed it. He contacted professionals but they charged by the hour, refusing to help him if he couldn't pay. Nothing he tried worked and he realised that people didn't really care unless there was some sort of favour or payment to be made in return. He lost faith in humanity, and soon enough, all adults became horrible, nasty animals. He was ready to give up until he was diagnosed with cancer. It was the one thing that saved him.

He started working on weekends as soon as he was able to and began to take measures to ensure he was able to save up and move out. If his life up until then taught him anything, it was the importance of protecting himself and his own wellbeing.

Sophia continued to read the words on the page as she wiped a tear that had begun to from her eyes.

Every dream begins with a dreamer. As long as your heart is beating, you will have time to make yours a reality. Everyone has a dream, but only you can make yours come true. Let me teach you how.

She put the pages down. She didn't need to read

any more. She loved the passion in Oliver, it was his way of words, his calmness and peacefulness that she adored most about him, along with everything else that made him who he was. He had a beautiful soul despite his abusive childhood, a soul so kind and so deep. Like everyone, he had bad times which resulted in his fair share of wrong doings, but he still came out kind, gentle and positive on the other side.

Whilst not even being in the same room as her, Oliver had inspired her for her next film. Sophia wiped her eyes and headed towards a shelf full of their favourite collection of films.

Next up was film number two. She picked out *The Green Mile*.

CHAPTER **SEVEN**

It was a quiet and cold Monday afternoon and an eerie atmosphere spread throughout the house. Oliver had left for work in the early hours of the morning, forgetting to turn on the heating for Sophia before his departure. Outside, the air was damp. The roads were wet from the rain that had fallen during the night and the sky was hidden behind a thin layer of silver clouds.

Sophia sat on the sofa with her grey blanket wrapped around her. The chill bit into her fingers and toes, ripping into her skin like a hungry wolf. Her muscles stiffened as its teeth pierced through her limbs, tearing them off one by one. Her legs were the first to go. She sat there, with her eyes smouldered in fury and hatred as nature beat her again, taking away her ability to run away, despite her legs still being intact.

The moisture in the air and the rain fall overnight had formed an invisible and slippery layer of mist over each of the radiant and fiery colours of the autumn leaves that that carpeted the footpath outside. Sophia had been left with no option but to turn back from her short escape, to avoid the risk of slipping on the new carpet that had threatened to pull her to the ground. Mother Nature had obstructed Sophia's remaining bit of freedom of temporarily being able to escape, trapping her in her own home.

It was nearly 9:30 a.m. and Sophia had been eating her breakfast whilst watching *Friends*. She'd spent a longer time in the shower, crying and washing away her thoughts of the nightmare before. It was just another thing that had become a part of her daily routine. Regardless of how often these nightmares and feelings would overcome her, she struggled to get used to the fear and pain they caused, despite having accepted her life and the emptiness that came with it.

She put down her bowl on the coffee table and walked out of the room as her thermal leggings and a long thick, camel colour, jumper-dress failed to keep her warm. She needed to move. Her hair was wet and wrapped in a towel, sending a bitterly cold shiver down the back of her neck. She moved up the steps, looking thin and stick-like. Her face was stripped of any colour that it once had. The rose that blushed from her cheeks, the pink that bounced from her lips and the orangey brown that sparkled deep within her eyes, had disappeared.

Sophia found herself to be standing at the entrance of the spare room. The room had once been their project haven, what others would call a 'home office'. It was a peaceful place where she and Oliver would carry out their little projects together.

It had been months since she was last in there. It wasn't a large room but was large enough to hold two work stations and a comfy brown sofa with a shelving cabinet against the wall, filled with inspirational quotes, books and various ornaments that they'd collected together from days out and holidays abroad.

The room was rectangular in shape and was located in the corner of the second floor of the house. Two small windows took up two of the walls in the room, one overlooking into the garden, and the other into the space between their home and their neighbour's home. This window had a beautiful hand painted image of a dusty-pink sky with its reflection glistening over the ocean. Sophia had painted it when they moved in, with glass paints to introduce a nicer and more colourful atmosphere into the room, and to block out the brick wall outside.

Together, Sophia and Oliver had carried out research into designing a room that bounced off positive vibrations to help set their minds into focusing on what they wanted in life. This was a room that had housed their motivation and pushed them to lean towards their dreams.

The walls were splashed with a browny-grey, stone paint, and a light beige carpet was spread across the floor. Paintings and ornaments of Ganesh, the Hindu God of beginnings, and of Buddha, symbolising wisdom and mindfulness, filled specific areas on the walls and shelves to create a sense of peace and tranquillity. A deep green, leafy plant stood tall beside a brown sofa that sat in the corner of the room, and a little ornament of a waterfall with three stone elephants sat on the window sill not too far from it.

The wall opposite the window that overlooked the garden, was home to a large mirror with the words 'Your true reflection is in your heart' frosted along the top. The mirror was one of the room's best features as it bounced sunlight across the walls, filling it with a boost of brightness and warmth. Scented candles were placed on little tables and shelves and were used in the evenings and during the darker months to create a deeper sense of relaxation. The room had been perfect; neat, clean, and so peaceful.

But it had been derelict for a few months now and had lost the atmosphere that it once held. Sophia stood there, looking around her. It was cold and dark. The curtains were half open, but light didn't want to enter. Clutter and boxes filled the room, dust settled on the tables, on the shelves and ornaments and the sense of peace and tranquillity had vanished. The working stations which had once been kept neat and tidy were now filled with junk. Today was the day this room was to become peaceful again. Sophia rolled up her sleeves. It was time to clear out the mess.

She walked toward the dark, stone coloured

curtains of the window closest to her overlooking the neighbours' house, and pulled the string as an attempt to welcome light into the room. It refused. It was dark outside and the dull and dusty ambience of the room remained. Sophia glared at the desk further away from her, by the other window that overlooked the long garden. Oliver's desk. A pile of papers were stacked in the corner – all the rough notes he had written prior to beginning his book. She walked to his desk, around the clutter on the floor and over the boxes. She ran her fingers along the desk, sweeping a line of dust at the same time as she moved closer to the pile of papers. She picked up a handful, taking a closer look.

The first line of his notes, an affirmation:

I'm doing this because this is my dream. You have to look after your dreams. You can do anything you set your mind to so don't let anyone tell you otherwise. Only you know your boundaries. I'm doing this for me, because I can, and I will.

It wasn't Oliver's parents who taught him follow his dreams. It was film. *A Happiness* was one film that carried a message that Oliver loved. It was so many things than just a film. It showed him how a man's weakness turned to strength, the power of hope when there's nothing else, the teaching that despite having nothing, a person can still have everything.

Oliver had always been determined, from the moment he could think clearly for himself. He knew the importance of happiness. He knew what he didn't want to be, and he knew what needed to be done to not end up like his dad. It was after his illness when he was able to really think about his life and what he wanted from it. He began to set real goals and truly focus on what steps he needed to take to get there. He made a timeline and promised himself to let go of the past and focus on building a better future, by following his passion to make himself happy.

I'm doing this for me, because I can, and I will.

Sophia read the line again and smiled as she held the page close to her body and closed her eyes, recalling the moment he wrote those exact words on the page, back when they first met.

***

Oliver had left the hospital with his mum after his first consultation with his doctor. His chemotherapy session was to take place in three weeks' time for six months followed by radiotherapy after three months of completing chemotherapy, followed by even more scans and tests. He was numb. His prayers of being taken from this world were finally being answered and in time, his parents would no longer need to carry the burden of having to feed him and put a roof over his head. Years, even a lifetime of feeling unwanted and being in the way of two people, were coming to an end. He walked out silently knowing he wasn't going to make it, not wanting to make it. He sighed in relief. It was going to be over soon.

For days Oliver would be quiet. He would lie in his bed every night, questioning his existence and wondering what he did so wrong to be treated and made to feel so worthless and hated. Every night, he'd be unable to fight back the tears while questioning why God choose him to die, and why now and not at birth. Questions of his existence and purpose filled his mind. Wherever he was, however he felt, even through the smallest moments of positivity, a reminder of his worthlessness and belonging crept through, dominating any other thought inside him.

Despite his problems at home, Oliver did right. At school he would focus on his work, he had many friends and would try to help whoever he felt needed it, giving away the love he wished he'd received at home. But after he was diagnosed with cancer, he dropped every value he held on to, giving up on being a good person to others and himself. He stopped caring about people and pushed away his friends. His mum tried to be around, but worked most of the time. It was Lucy's Aunty who would take him to and from hospital. Lucy's Aunty never minded. Although she was physically there for him, mentally, Oliver had no-one and was left to go through his illness alone.

It was only when he started his chemotherapy when he began to see differently. He'd speak to other patients going through illnesses. Some had been diagnosed on a number of occasions while others were like Oliver, and were there for the first time. There wasn't a set criteria on age, gender or who or where they were in life. It wasn't about your background or upbringing, where they worked and how rich or poor they were. All of those who were there, were there for the same reason. They shared the same fear and the same illness and for the first time in his life, Oliver felt like he belonged.

The only one difference between Oliver and the other patients was that their fear was of dying. They valued their lives and wanted to live, while Oliver intended not to stay.

Oscar, a middle-aged man was at the hospital most of the times that Oliver was there. He had a son of similar age to Oliver and spoke about him with such love and positivity. Oscar would speak to Oliver, and share with him the same positivity he would tell his own children, about life, and happiness. He would share stories of his two sons Liam and Ben, and his wife, Elizabeth. He'd once asked Oliver what he planned to do once his treatment was over, once he was given a second chance at life. Oliver had shrugged, like any other child. He'd only ever imaged darkness in his future.

One night, despite feeling weak and sick, Oliver found himself staring into the mirror, looking for himself. A young boy stared back at him. He didn't recognise him. He never did know who he was and what he wanted out of life. He thought long and hard for days, weeks even, throughout and after his chemotherapy.

As months went on, Oliver began to observe people whilst at the hospital, their faces, their reactions to illnesses, and the effects on those around them. He'd begun to value his life and the people he'd met during his times in and out of hospital. The people who spread joy and positivity, who showed him that there was so much more to life, who made him realise how big the world was outside of the four walls of his room. Then there were the people who spread sadness and negativity, who wrote down a bucket list of things they wished they did, trying to set unrealistic goals to cram in experiences over such a short period, in desperation to fulfil the dreams they never knew they had. And then those who had been fighting for too long and had already given up. Oliver was grateful to have met them all.

It was Oscar who had given Oliver a new lens to look through. His thoughts were different, positive. Even if it was for a brief moment of his life, Oliver was beginning to see a flicker of light in his future, and for the first time, he felt like he had a dad. But Oscar was taken away from him when his family decided to move out of town, down south closer to the coast. Although Oscar had left his number with the nurse to give to Oliver, Oliver didn't have a phone to contact him on, nor did he want to impose on Oscar's new life.

He'd found his inspiration in his new dad and

decided he wanted to spread happiness and positivity into others the way Oscar had done for him. He'd imagine Oscar sometimes, even today, sitting by the sea, staring out, watching the waves, happily with his family. It made him feel warm despite missing him.

When Oliver was well enough to go back to school in year seven, he became a new person. His values of being helpful and kind came back stronger and he'd developed a new passion for using his experiences to live every day as if it was his last.

It was these words that Oscar had drilled into him during their talks at the hospital, and these words that Oliver had stuck by ever since. He wanted to spread the kindness to those who needed it most. He wanted to be there, like Oscar was there for him, for those in need of help but didn't have the courage to ask for it. He wanted to write a book, and even though his parents disagreed with it, Oliver took his second chance and began to create a new life for no-one other than himself.

It was Sophia's first day at Totham High School. She and her mum had moved to the Northford area just outside London, following her dad's death. Sophia had no friends or family around her and it was a mare decision based on the first location her mum was able to find full-time work.

It was lunchtime and Oliver had been sat in the playground at a table on his own, with a notepad and pen. It was also his first day back at school. Lucy, who had befriended Sophia the moment she walked into the classroom, had gone over to Oliver in the playground to introduce the new girl.

'Oli, this is Sophia, she's new and today's her first day. Sophia, this is Oliver.' Lucy took a seat opposite Oliver. Sophia sat beside Lucy and smiled. Oliver smiled back and went back to his notepad.

Lucy and Oliver talked together while Sophia listened, unsure of whether she should be listening, and unsure of what to say. It seemed like a personal conversation and she didn't know Oliver. She was also shy and still not over the loss of her dad and wasn't comfortable in hearing about Oliver's experiences in hospital. To keep herself pre-occupied, Sophia had looked at Oliver's notepad whilst he spoke to Lucy.

I'm doing this because this is my dream. You have to look after your dreams. You can do anything you set your mind to so don't let anyone tell you otherwise. Only you know your boundaries. I'm doing this for me, because I can, and I will.

Oliver caught Sophia's eyes on his notepad and closed it. She looked away slightly embarrassed to have been caught being nosey upon the first instance of meeting someone.

'Have you seen it?' he asked.

'Sorry?' Sophia blushed over being called her out on looking at what he'd written in his notepad.

'*A Happiness.* Have you seen it, or read the book?' he continued.

She nodded. Sophia had never been confident when it came to talking around new people but having been caught looking at his personal book made her feel that much more uncomfortable.

'You have nothing, but if you're happy, that's enough, and you have everything. That's what we should live for - happiness.' Oliver got up and walked away with his notepad and book.

Sophia turned to Lucy, who smiled and shrugged. 'That's Ol,' Lucy giggled. Sophia smiled back.

Neither of the three knew at this point, that this was just the beginning of a friendship of a lifetime.

***

Sophia put down the notes, smiling to herself. 'We had some good memories Ol,' she said as she walked over to the other end of the table. A heavy laptop sat on the left side of the table beside a little red book that caught her eye. Sophia had seen the book before. She'd recognised it from her days in sixth form – *The Lord of the Flies*. Oliver had bought it for her on her twenty fifth birthday, knowing how fond she was of the book. She smiled and flicked though the pages, reminiscing back to her English classes years ago. She came across one of her favourite parts of the book and skimmed through it whilst taking a seat on a pyramid of boxes that were piled up beside the desk.

It was a conversation between two of the characters. The scapegoat of the book, who was constantly being bullied and picked on, had been giving another young boy the courage and strength to carry on. Sophia took a deep breath and released slowly. This was the moment in the book where hope was beginning to distance itself from two of the children, where reality, fear and tiredness settled in. The conversation was so powerful, portraying the impacts of one person's positive or negative behaviour onto another. Sophia and Oliver had read the book together once, and Oliver had shared his own insight to this particular section, using his own experiences. Sophia closed her eyes, taking herself there as they lay together on the sofa, reading and talking. She smiled and felt warm as she heard his voice.

'I like this part too Soph. When you care so much for something but everyone around you doesn't, eventually you lose the will to care too. It takes one person to ignite the flame inside to help pursue your aim, and in this story, it was the courage and positivity of the scapegoat. It was because of him that the other boys decided to carry on and not give up hope. Because yes, what would that mean for the rest of humanity if everyone was to give up and stop caring? That's why in life, when things get tough, you just have to carry on.'

Sophia opened her eyes, still feeling Oliver's warmth around her.

'When things get tough, you just have to carry on,' she said as she sighed. She paused and stood still in the room before releasing the false strength she was holding on to, letting the reality hit her. 'We just have to carry on,' she repeated. Sophia took another deep breath and exhaled abruptly as she stood up from her new chair of boxes. She was not weak and she was not giving up. She stood, ready to face the memories and fight the battle of cleaning the spare room.

'I will go on,' she whispered underneath her breath as she smiled and walked towards a CD player that sat on the shelving unit. She knew what CD was in there. She took a deep breath before hitting the play button. Bob Marley, *Is This Love?* played through the speakers. Sophia found an area in the centre of the room and closed her eyes, swaying from side to side as she listened. She listened to Oliver as he sang to her gently in her ears as they lay together on the living room sofa of their university apartment. She felt the love in his voice as he sang each word, whilst telling her of their future together through his eyes, and how much he loved her through his touch. She wrapped her arms around herself as though she was being comforted by Oliver's embrace. She swayed and smiled, with her eyes closed, gently moving from side to side to the song, going right back to the moment where he had first sung to her, and re-living it from deep within.

Silence filled the air as the song came to an end. Sophia stood, still wrapped in Oliver's embrace with her eyes closed. For a moment, the feeling of love and happiness surrounded her. There she was, standing back in the peaceful room again, filled with all the good things they loved, doing all the things they'd been dreaming of since forever. She and Oliver had taken a break from their creativities one time, and had danced together, slowly, in the small space to *Is This Love?* the same way Sophia had been doing now.

Sophia opened her eyes and as if almost instantly, the feeling of happiness became distant.

'I will go on,' she whispered, once again allowing herself to take in the inspiration from Oliver and *The Lord of the Flies*. Sophia walked back towards the CD player to press the repeat button. Something shimmered in the corner of her eye, distracting her away from playing their song.

On the shelf, not far from the CD player was a long and thick candle that had never been lit. Sophia moved towards the candle, picking it up gently. She bought it up to her nose and the scent of cinnamon filled her nostrils. It smelt as strong as it did when she first bought it years ago when she moved into Oliver's flat after they got married.

Oliver had moved out of his parents' home as soon as he was able to afford paying rent. He packed his necessities and walked out, ready to start a new life for himself. He'd kept in contact with his mum but over time, both had drifted apart.

Sophia didn't have the heart to leave her mum and refused to live elsewhere despite having been with Oliver for such a long time. They took turns now and again, staying at each other's homes but it wasn't until after their autumn wedding when Sophia finally agreed to move into Oliver's flat. But on weekends Sophia would go back home for the sake of her mum, as much as Isabella refused for her daughter to go back home for her. It wasn't until Isabella retired and decided to leave and go to Spain for twelve months to stay with her sister, when Sophia truly began to see Oliver's flat as their own home. A cinnamon scented candle with the words 'Home isn't a place, it's a feeling,' engraved into a metal holder at the bottom was the first item she'd purchased for the flat when she finally believed it to be her home.

Sophia put the candle down and turned towards the CD player. She pressed the repeat button before walking back to the table to sift through the rest of its contents. The sound of Bob Marley's voice filled the air as it played again.

A beautiful and heavy stone the size of her palm was placed on top of Sophia's old art pad. The stone was big and thick and was carved finely into the shape of a heart. Layers of brown and red grains created patterns within the stone which had been smoothed out and glazed over with gloss. It was a gift that Oliver had bought back for Sophia from the Grand Canyon when he went on holiday for two weeks in spring with some of his friends. It was their first time apart and the first time Sophia realised exactly how much Oliver meant to her.

Every morning and every night, during every day to day movement, everything had reminded her of him. The sunshine, the smell of freshly cut grass, the vibrant green in the leaves of the trees, even the yellow daffodils that grew in the flower beds along the pavements in the streets. Anything yellow, anything that represented happiness and brightness had reminded her of Oliver and how much she couldn't wait for him to get back. She'd send him text messages now and again, trying hard not to distract him or overdo it to a point where he was unable to enjoy his holiday. She'd heard of clingy girlfriends and she definitely didn't want to be one of them. She'd sometimes force herself not to send him messages so he could enjoy his time with his friends without constantly being on the phone messaging her. She'd imagine he was with her, and imagine she'd told him whatever it was she wanted to say, that way she wouldn't need to send him text messages every hour about silly things that weren't important. Regardless, however, Oliver always text her back and sent her photos. He missed her just as much.

This heart stone was so much more than a heart stone, it held so much love within it and represented so much more. It represented their love for each other and their experiences away from each other. It wasn't something Sophia would ever have been able to forget. In her eyes, having that heart meant having Oliver, and being close to him. It was the most valuable item anyone had ever given her and she treasured it.

Sophia picked it up and stroked her fingers along

the compressed grains within the stone. It was still just as smooth as it was when she had first received it, glazed and colourful, with various layers of dark browns and dusty reds. She held it tightly in her hand, holding it up to her heart as she closed her eyes for a moment before putting it back on the table beside her art pad.

She placed a finger on her art pad and paused for a second before flicking through it. It was filled with sketches of colourful elephants, lions and tigers – some of Sophia's favourite animals. On the last page, was a drawing of a panda coloured in different shades of yellows, blues and greens. It was a rough sketch that she had drawn for Oliver with the intention of painting it on canvas as part of his birthday present, but Sophia never got around to doing it. She put the art pad down on the table and smiled. Oliver would have loved it.

Beside the art pad, there was a receipt from a large vehicle hire company that was based not too far from her mum's house. Sophia felt a gust of cold air instantly fill the space around her as the snakes suddenly began to wrap around her stomach in their sleep, taking comfort in squeezing her insides. A sense of uneasiness crept upon her like vines entwining around a tree. She picked up the receipt and the piece of paper that was stapled to it with the words 'Lorry Hire' printed across the top. She felt her insides contract harder as the taste of vomit filled her mouth. Another sign? She turned to the stack of boxes that she had been sitting on before, moving her attention towards the more positive items in the room, moving away from the truth.

The box at the top of the pile wasn't sealed. Inside, were her winter clothes, neatly folded and packed away. A fluffy, baby pink jumper lay on the top. It was the one she wore when they first moved into the house together. It was the same jumper that Oliver had picked out for her when they went away to Scotland on their first holiday together.

***

They'd gone just before Christmas, for Oliver's birthday. It was a spur of the moment thing, which was out of character for Oliver but still something that he agreed to do regardless. They wanted to go away together, after their university courses were over and had planned to get away by going on a road trip to Scotland, failing to think about the complications of snow in December. They'd organised everything within days and had agreed to pack minimal as to not weigh down the car or have to carry too much. They had their route planned, their breaks, and places to sleep along the way. Everything had been planned perfectly, everything except for any disruptions caused by the weather in Scotland in December.

It had snowed on their first day up and continued to throughout. One of the nights was so bad, that they ended up stranded, along with hundreds of other drivers along a long, hilly road. The snow had settled and was still coming down fast and heavy. They had no choice but to leave the car parked on the side of the road behind a trail of other cars that had been stuck. Sophia and Oliver slept in the back of their car for the night. Oliver held Sophia close, keeping her warm as she tried not to shiver. They lay together, keeping busy and deterring their thoughts away from the situation, telling each other riddles and playing music off their phones in the background until they fell asleep using each other's body heat to stay warm. Oliver had fallen asleep first. The moonlight shone on his face and Sophia had spent hours watching him. His face was beautiful and she couldn't help but look at him as he lay peacefully, his face so relaxed and so innocent. He was perfect.

They woke up the next morning to the sun beaming into the car. Its heat, the brightness outside and the view of immaculate snow covering the hills on each side made the moment even more romantic than the night before.

It had taken a while for the cars to start clearing out, but eventually they did and Sophia and Oliver were able to continue with their journey. It had still been a long, cold and uncomfortable night, and they were hungry after forgetting to pack any food to keep in the car.

'And that's why I have to plan. This last minute stuff doesn't seem to be working does it Soph?' Oliver had said as they searched for a supermarket.

'Shut up Ol, last night was nice. And you slept well, snoring so hard I thought an elephant had joined us.' Sophia joked and held his hand as he drove, raising it to her lips to give it a kiss. Oliver squeezed her hand and smiled.

'It was an elephant. I don't snore,' he joked back.

After few miles of driving, they stopped off at a café for breakfast. The café was connected to a large supermarket where they went after breakfast, to stock up on snacks and water to keep in the car in case of another snow episode.

A baby pink jumper, fluffy and cosy-looking, hung in the clothes section that they'd been walking past to get further into the store. Oliver picked it out for Sophia, remembering how cold she had been the night before. There was a baby blue one and a camel coloured one too, and although she preferred the camel colour, she'd stuck with Oliver's choice and bought the pink one.

***

Sophia picked up the jumper and held it close to her as she scanned around the rest of the room. A tiny little book sat on the shelving unit, around eight centimeters in height and width with the word 'Soulmates,' printed across the cover. Sophia walked over to the shelving unit and picked up the mini book without hesitation, skimming through it while reading some of the pages. She'd come across it one time in a card shop and flicked through it randomly. It wasn't the usual kind of book she would pick up to flick through but something about this caught her attention and lured her into taking a closer look. From just flicking though, she found herself standing in the store, turning to the front page and reading each page thoroughly, surprised at how she was able to relate to every single word. As cheesy as it was, it made her smile and love Oliver that much more, and so she purchased the book to gift to him.

She turned to the back of the book where her own handwritten words were neatly placed:

I loved you yesterday, I love you today, I'll love you tomorrow. Forever.

She smiled and ran her fingers along her writing. Nearly seventeen years on and her words still remained true.

Four hours had passed and Sophia had looked at everything in the room thoroughly. Positive and happy memories surrounded her. She walked back towards the door and stood by the corner for a final inspection. She looked around, at all the clutter that was scattered along the desks, shelves and within the boxes. She was surrounded by memories from every step of their relationship. This wasn't clutter, this wasn't mess. This was love, and each object in the room represented a different, happy memory. There wasn't anything there for Sophia to clean up. This room was filled with love.

She took another deep breath, looked around and closed her eyes. She exhaled, and inhaled again, deeply breathing in and out, feeling the warmth of love within the room. She opened her eyes and took another look around before smiling to herself. She turned to the door and left the room.

Sophia walked into the bedroom, removing the towel from her head. Her hair was still damp from having it wrapped in a towel for so long but she refused to dry it. The feeling of happiness relaxed her, making her want to sleep peacefully as she hoped the feeling would continue through into her dreams. She climbed onto Oliver's side of the bed and curled up into a ball on top of the bedsheets. She looked at the time on the clock that sat facing her on the bedside table. It was 5:30 p.m. There was still some time before Oliver was to reach home. She lay there and closed her eyes. This time she wasn't forcing herself to stay awake, and she wasn't stopping herself from crying. This time she was content. A small smile appeared on her face as she relaxed her body where Oliver would usually lay. She closed her eyes and began falling into deep sleep.

CHAPTER **EIGHT**

Sophia sat in the park, just outside Lilly's. She sat on a bench overlooking the pond, watching the bubbles form at the bottom of the fountain in the centre. She watched the small ripples glide across the pond until they disappeared. She watched as the flock of birds danced together in the skies, and watched as the trees swayed gently with them. A lady with an empty pushchair walked by slowly and a little girl waddled a few steps behind, staring at Sophia and smiling sweetly. A man walking his dog strolled by a few moments later and nodded at Sophia.

'Morning,' he greeted her and she smiled back.

The birds continued to dance and the trees continued to sway. The sun continued to shine on Sophia's face. It was right above her, shining through the dancing trees. The peaceful sound of the water filled her ears and the sun's warmth embraced her face as she looked up, smiling with her eyes closed. She was at peace, so calm, so grateful and in a happy place.

The lady with the pushchair walked past Sophia again, slowly. Sophia opened her eyes and watched as the little girl followed a few steps behind, staring at Sophia, smiling sweetly. The man walking his dog strolled by again a few moments later and nodded at her.

'Morning,' he greeted her. Her smile began to fade. The same birds continued to dance and the trees continued to sway. The sun continued to shine on Sophia but the atmosphere began to feel different.

She sat and waited as she observed her surroundings. She didn't know what she was waiting for. But something was strange. The ripples from the pond continued to glide across the water until they disappeared. The birds danced in the skies and the trees swayed along with them. She sat there, looking around her. The lady with the pushchair walked by again, slowly, and the little girl followed behind as she stared at Sophia, smiling. The man walking his dog strolled by a few moments later and nodded at her.

'Morning,' he greeted her once again.

The light faded from their eyes as they became dark and heavy. Whatever *it* was, they were in on it. Sophia was out of her trance. The peace she felt seconds ago had turned into fear as the moment continued to go on as though it was on loop. The birds, the trees, the lady with the pushchair, the child walking behind her, the man, his dog, they continued to go around in circles, teasing her, playing, teaming up with the man with the blurred face, all set to torture Sophia into seeing the truth. Sophia closed her eyes in disbelief; her dream was becoming another nightmare.

The hard sound of a thump awoke her from her thoughts and she opened her eyes. A bird lay on the ground beside her. Another thump and another bird fell from the sky. Then another, and another, until they all surrounded her, dying on the park floor. Sophia looked up. The trees had stopped swaying and the park had become still. The fountain had stopped. The old man, his dog and the lady and her child had vanished. Only Sophia was there, but she wasn't alone. She began to recite numbers, counting as an attempt to calm her nerves. One. Two. Three. The air around her let off a sense of danger as a dark cloud closed in over the pond's reflection. But the sky was clear. Four. Sophia kept her eyes on the pond, glaring as the water became darker, deeper. An air bubble popped in the centre as it rose to the top. The fountain started up. Five. The snakes began to slither inside her, starved and hungry, opening their mouths as they prepared to bite, putting an end to her nightmare. Six. Seven. Sophia watched in horror as she witnessed thick, red liquid begin to pour from the fountain as the pond slowly filled with blood. She stopped counting.

The sound of screaming tore through Sophia's ears

like shards of glass. The screams began to get louder and sharper as they pierced into her head, surging through her skull, stabbing into the part of her brain where all of her bad memories were stored as they spilled out like a malicious and deadly virus. Her heart pumped desperately, trying to survive the infection that was spreading through Sophia's mind. She looked around, unaware of where the screams were coming from. They had to be stopped, but there was no cure. She recognised the screams. They were screams of hysteria and panic, of disbelief, bordering on terror. She'd heard them before and knew them too well. They were hers.

The gentle ripples across the pond transformed into angry waves, with one wave fighting against the other. The sounds of blood crashing against each other grew louder, as if competing with the sounds of her screams. Blood began to overflow, spilling onto the surrounding grassy areas. She knew someone was there, watching. She could feel him, glaring at her with a psychotic look in his eyes, taking pleasure in her suffering, using it to fuel his next move. The pond began to stretch, slowly as it moved towards Sophia. The sound of the blood pouring from the fountain got louder and louder. The snakes inside her began to bite, piercing their fangs into her as they punctured her soul. She tried to stand but a force held her down firmly onto the bench, making her numb with shock. The snakes inside her had bitten hard, spilling venom though her veins, fast and vicious like a tsunami in a storm. They were in on it too. She was paralysed. Her heart was beating rapidly. The echoes of her screaming and the cries of the dying birds that surrounded her began to fill the air. The waves crashing, the blood seeping down the fountain, her screams and all of the other nasty sounds around her were contending against each other, fighting to be the loudest in her ears. The noises were deafening.

Sophia had to run but she was helpless. She couldn't move. She tried to close her eyes and take herself away to a safer place, but the force was too strong. This invisible power made her stay and watch although she didn't want to see. This meerkat wasn't ready to surrender but with no ability to run or hide, she had no option but to sit there and wait until the beast was ready to rip into her, tearing her into shreds, removing chunks of her life, and eating her alive.

Sophia looked down. Her feet were bare and emerged within the thick pool of warm, red, blood. She wanted to scream but she couldn't move.

Silence. The fountain stopped. The cries of the birds, her screams and the crashes of the waves of blood had all become silent. The pond now a large ocean of red and Sophia was seated in the centre, powerless and on display like a circus animal. The air was filled with nothingness. She sat there and watched, waiting for something to happen. Her heart began to feel nervous as it filled with anxiety and fear. Her limbs began to tingle with weakness as she waited. She felt sick.

But still nothing. Nothing was happening. She was being forced to watch, still unable to move or blink. Everything stood still apart from the sweat that trickled down Sophia's face. Something in the air had changed. A feeling of darkness took over her body, the air around her became eerie and dead. This was it. She knew it. Something was going to happen, today. Right now. This was the end. Even the voices inside her head hid away in terror, submerged within her brain, refusing to warn her.

Something moved in the distance. Beyond the fountain, a figure began to emerge. The sound of her heartbeat echoed in her ears and rippled throughout her body. The taste of sickness filled her mouth and throat as her stomach tightened. She tried to scream but nothing came out. There was nothing she could do. She watched, as this figure came closer and closer towards her. He was wearing muddy blue jeans and an unzipped, dark brown bomber jacket over a navy-blue hoodie. His hood was up, head down, and eyes staring right at her. Sophia tried to close her eyes – no luck. This was it. This was the end.

***

It was nearly 9:00 p.m. and Sophia had overslept. She lay in bed. Confused. Scared. She lay there, trying to make something of yet another nightmare. This wasn't like any other nightmare, where in all the others, she was able to run. This time, she had nothing. There was a power of some sort, and with each nightmare, it became stronger, taking away her ability to run or hide. It was only a matter of time now, she knew it. And there was nothing she could do.

Sophia took a deep breath, sighing as she looked at the time. Oliver was downstairs. He would have made his own dinner and eaten it on his own by now. She pictured him on his own, cooking, eating and washing up alone. Soon enough he would come up to bed, tired and ready to fall asleep, on his own, while she'd be awake. Another night without conversation, another night, together, but alone.

Sophia sighed again. It was too dark for her to get out and run away from her new nightmare. The only thing she could think of doing was to find a place where no-one would see or hear her so she could lock herself up and release her inner emotions. Her muscles remained limp as she forced herself out of bed, dragging herself into the bathroom like an addict in need of drugs. She turned on shower, letting the sound of falling water fill her ears. She sat on the floor in the corner of the room as her tears began to fall free. The voices inside her head hid away, filling the area of emptiness deep inside her, allowing her to have her moment of relief. She sat there, pitying herself, eyes closed as she waited for the steam to create mist over the mirrors and tiles, unable to look at her reflection, hating the person who would be staring back at her. Weak, pathetic, worthless Sophia.

It was 10:30 p.m. and Oliver had gone to bed. He lay there, still and peaceful, in deep sleep. Sophia fought the urge to wake him, she needed him to hold her, and tell her he loved her, and reassure her that everything would be okay. But instead she gave him a kiss on the forehead and turned back to make her way out of their room and down the stairs. She felt lost and alone. She hated how easy it was for him to fall asleep at night.

Sophia switched on the small lamp on the table beside the sofa in the living room. The space around it was dim and the shadows closed in around her. More sheets of paper sat on the table opposite her – Oliver's book. She leaned forward to reach for the pages and took a small handful before sitting back into the sofa, making herself comfortable, as she snuggled alone, underneath the fluffy, grey blanket.

She flicked through the pages in her hand. They had been typed up and edited with scribbles and mark-ups on every page. Sophia turned to a random page and began to read.

I don't know what the future holds, no-one does. We can try and make it, and we can try and shape it, but at the end of the day, whatever is meant to be will be, and we must accept it.

You can make your timeline. You can set your goals. You

could grow up with your friends and talk of the future, having dinners together with your partner and their partners, playdates with the kids whilst sipping on coffee and eating cake. You can make plans to do things together, and just continue to experience life's journey and grow together.

You're close, so close to having all of that but something happens and an invisible distance is created. It's there but only you know it. And it just grows further and further, and still, only you can see it. Over time you begin to distance yourself, because you realise you're no longer that person anymore. While everyone is moving forward, you're stuck on standstill. Everyone around you begins to seem like a stranger. Your future hopes and plans seem almost delusional and unrealistic. How stupid and wrong of you, to think it would be a happy ending. You're in your own bubble, not floating, but trapped, choking inside without any air, and your safety net has been taken away from you, because life's circumstances has changed you in such a way, you yourself don't know who you are anymore.

Cold air crawled up Sophia's legs and down her back like a spider, creeping on the delicate tips of his thin legs. She adjusted the blanket, covering any gaps but the coldness remained. She frowned as she turned to the next page of Oliver's work in progress, wondering if he had been writing his self-help book to help himself all these years. It would make sense considering the amount of torture he'd faced throughout his life. The taste of bitter coffee filled her mouth as it leaked from within her soul as she the thought of Oliver writing about their relationship crossed her mind. The voices inside her head began to whisper quietly, as if afraid of the eight legged creature that was moving in on her. So much had changed over the years, so much that hadn't been what they'd initially dreamt of. She began to get lost in her thoughts, suspicious of what he had been hiding from her, trying to think back and understand what could have happened to make him feel like he was stuck, annoyed at how he was certain that there would be no happy ending. She continued to read, in search for the answers she already had.

It may seem tough, heart-breaking, sad or disappointing, it may fill you with anger and resentment, it may make you make the wrong decisions and do wrong things, but in the end, there will be light. Once you're in the tunnel, you have to keep walking through. It sounds easy. It isn't. But it's important to try. It's important to try and remember that this is just another bump in the road. Accidents happen, and that's exactly what it will be, an accident. It's better, although not easy, to leave the damage at the scene of the crime, and move on. How do you know it won't be a happy ending? If you're not happy, it's not the end. No matter the situation, you have one life – make it count, and don't let anyone come in your way.

Sophia was confused. The spider had created a web, wrapping her up in a beautiful, silk parcel of questions. Questions that she'd hidden deep within the box and ones that she didn't want to know the answers to. The hissing of the snakes inside her head began to get louder, angrier as she continued to ignore the signs.

She shivered as she felt her insides drown in ice water like an unsinkable ship. The voices inside her head continued to hiss at her as she stood, wondering why he wasn't happy, asking herself what went wrong, undermining her role as his wife, focusing on her failures and insecurities, wishing she was good enough. Sophia sat and questioned whether Oliver was truly as happy as he made out to be. She questioned whether she was as happy as she thought she was. She couldn't tell. Somewhere along the road of their relationship, they had taken a wrong turn and neither of them seemed to know where they were heading.

The spider bit into her skin and crawled away, fast, leaving Sophia with a prickly sensation on her skin. A punishment for not listening to the signs.

'You have one life – make it count, and don't let anyone come in your way… Accidents happen, and that's exactly what it will be, an accident.'

She read the words over and over, before closing her eyes, taking herself back to nearly seven months ago.

CHAPTER NINE

It was a hot Saturday evening in March 2017, and Sophia and Oliver had called Tristan and Lucy over for dinner to celebrate Lucy's thirty-fifth birthday, a month later than her actual birthday.

Oliver had decorated the living room with a few balloons and birthday banners and put out a bottle of champagne with four champagne flutes. Sophia had cooked Tristan's favourite Indian dish; an egg curry with vegetable fried rice and homemade garlic naan bread. It was a dish she'd learned to make from Isabella who was taught by their Indian neighbours in their old home town. She also put together a large bowl of vegetable cous-cous, with an egg and avocado salad for Lucy, who had specifically stated she wanted something light and healthy but filling, with no spice or onions. Oliver had prepared his favourite dessert, a chocolate salted caramel cheesecake for himself and the others, and a special chocolate cheesecake for Sophia who wasn't keen on salted caramel.

Oliver, Tristan and Lucy were catching up in the living room, teasing each other like old times whilst Sophia set the dining table and heated the dinner.

'You really didn't need to go through all the trouble Soph, honestly, Tristan would have been more than happy with the cous-cous, and you know I've never been bothered about birthdays,' Lucy walked into the kitchen.

Tristan and Lucy had got together soon after Sophia and Oliver. It was when they were leaving sixth form to go to university when Lucy realised it was time to tell Tristan how she felt, despite being so desperately against relationships. Initially, Tristan had refused to listen, not wanting anything to get in the way of their friendship. It came to him as a shock, especially knowing that Lucy was anti-relationships. But after a while, he realised it was Lucy he wanted. They'd moved in together a year later, renting out a flat near Tristan's university. Lucy had dropped out of her nursing course at her university to be closer to him and started working full-time practicing as a social worker whilst studying at the same time. After Tristan had graduated three years later, his parents bought him a small house nearby, where he and Lucy lived together. Tristan proposed on Christmas Day two years later, and they married the following year in May, four years before Sophia and Oliver.

'Seriously Soph, you really didn't need to make so much effort,' Lucy repeated.

Lucy never celebrated her birthday. She'd lost her mum who died whilst she was giving birth to Lisa, Lucy's younger twin sister, who she also lost that day. Her dad, and everyone else in the family never did find their birthday an occasion to be celebrating. Over the years, it became normal and it wasn't something that bothered Lucy. But when her older sister, Ivy, passed away from cancer when she was just thirteen years old, Lucy's life had changed. Her dad was unable to cope and Lucy was left to be taken care of by her Aunty, who had two children of her own to think about.

Lucy sat at the dining table, twirling a strand of hair around her fingers. 'I remember back in sixth form, when you all bought me that locket. I still have it you know. I have everything,' Lucy smiled as she continued to play with her hair. Sophia had picked up a silver heart locket that opened up. Inside were the photos of two babies, one was Lucy and the other Lisa. Lucy never wore jewellery but that was the best gift she had ever received.

'You know I cried the second I got home.' She giggled, embarrassed for admitting she had feelings. 'I still can't tell you how much that meant to me, how much it still means to me.' She smiled at Sophia who had been flapping around the cooker.

Sophia felt content and warm as she lifted the lid of the egg curry to give it a final stir before taking it off the heat. The aroma moved through the house, reminding her of her old house, in her old town when Isabella would cook egg curry for her dad.

'Smells so good Soph!' Tristan called from the living room. He walked into the kitchen seconds after. He took the lid off the pan, releasing the fragrances again, of all of the spices from within the curry. He inhaled as he let the scent of curry leaves, cinnamon and turmeric, fill his nostrils.

'Mmmm. You know me too well,' he laughed, happily closing the lid before heading towards the sink to wash his hands.

'Ol tells me you've agreed to celebrate your birthday for once. Off to Lake Como in two days eh?' Tristan turned off the tap and walked over to Sophia to give her a high five.

Instead, Sophia smiled and gave him a hand towel and left the kitchen to call Oliver who had picked up the unopened bottle of champagne and the four flutes to bring to the table. Dinner was ready.

'Right, who's ready to pop the champagne?' Oliver had pointed a champagne flute at Lucy.

Sophia had now bought all of the food to the table along with cutlery and took her seat opposite Lucy.

'Birthday girl?' Oliver walked over to Lucy placing the flute down, ready to open the bottle.

'Wait Ol, sit down first, Tristan has something to say.' Lucy turned to Oliver and put her hand on the bottle, pushing it down slightly to stop him from opening it.

'Tristan?' Lucy turned to him, shyly.

Tristan took his seat beside Lucy and Oliver walked over to Sophia, taking his place beside her.

'Okay, before I say anything, just a quick thank you both for all of this, honestly, you guys are amazing. The best friends and family right here.' Tristan had been nervously shaking his leg underneath the table. This was all too serious for him.

'Come on T, you're beginning to sound like Ol ten years ago,' Lucy smiled as she put her hand on Tristan's knee, patting it slowly to calm him. The others laughed.

'Lucy's pregnant.' Tristan announced, quickly and straight to the point, but also proudly, as he held her hand on his knee underneath the table, tightly.

'Oh wow!' Sophia screamed in excitement, 'I'm going to be an Aunty!'

'And I'm going to be an Uncle! Uncle Oli! This is amazing!' Oliver had a big grin on his face.

'Double celebration today, more of a reason to open this bottle!' he exclaimed.

Sophia and Oliver walked around the table to congratulate the couple. Oliver grabbed Tristan's hand, pulling him closer for a hug.

'Congratulations T,' he laughed joyfully as he put his other arm around Tristan. Oliver was truly so excited.

He moved over to Lucy and embraced her, still with the bottle of champagne in his hand, too excited to notice. For the first time, Oliver didn't know what to say to her. He was immensely ecstatic that Lucy's life was working out for her, better than she had thought.

'Now, let's not get emotional. We're here to celebrate Lucy's birthday, and Sophia's too seeing as you'll be in Como for it?' Tristan sat back down in his chair and Sophia made her way back to hers.

'No, just Lucy's today,' Oliver replied as he took away one of the flutes from the table and walked over to the fridge. 'Sorry, but Sophia's celebrating her birthday for the first time in twenty-four years, so no sharing, and it starts with Lake Como.' He continued talking whilst rummaging through the fridge, placing the champagne flute on the unit beside it. 'We'll be back on the fifteenth, the day after her birthday so we'll do something else after that.' Oliver walked back over to the table with a bottle of cloudy lemonade – one of Lucy's favourite soft drinks.

'Fair enough,' Tristan nodded at Sophia continuously, smiling. He was thrilled that Sophia had finally agreed to look ahead and celebrate her birthday.

'Baby names!' Sophia called out ecstatically, moving the conversation back to Lucy. Sophia loved children. She'd always wanted to be a mother, to have a tiny baby and love and cherish it forever. Before she met Oliver, she'd never thought she'd have her own, it was never going to be possible. She'd have to be with someone she truly loved, and after seeing what her mum went through after her dad's death, she would never have let herself love anyone. She'd thought about adopting and fostering but soon realised it wouldn't be fair on the child. She would have wanted to give her child everything, but she couldn't see him or her being happy with just Sophia, going to school and have other children talk about their mum and dad, whilst this child only had her, who wasn't even their real mum. She didn't want to be the reason for a child to ever feel unwanted or unloved, so she accepted her fate.

It took a long time for Sophia to come around to it, even whilst she was with Oliver. The thought of him leaving her or changing as a person and the impact it would have on a child put her off. But as the years went on, she began to get more and more attracted to Oliver, both physically and mentally, and their relationship grew stronger. She realised that she may get her own family after all. Being with Oliver made her see things differently. It made her feel the importance and powerful strength behind the impacts of what could be and how much you could do when you're with someone who truly loves you and wants the best for you. There was nothing stopping her from letting her walk towards where she wanted to be. She did want to be a mother, and at that moment, right there at the table around her best friends, she realised she was ready.

'Ahh Soph, if I could name her after you I would, but two Sophia's would be confusing.' Lucy smiled as she put a spoon of cous-cous into her mouth.

She genuinely meant it. Lucy had loved Sophia's name, and she loved her as a person too. She looked up to Sophia and had always seen her as a sister, a more calm and relaxed sister who had all her shit together.

'So, it's a girl?' Sophia asked. Everyone turned to Lucy, even Tristan, raising his eyebrows as if to ask, 'how do you know?'

'Ha ha, I am only two days into my pregnancy and apparently it's too early to tell,' Lucy blushed. 'But I think you'll have a niece, let's call it a mother's instinct?'

'I guess we'll find out in nine months' time! November right? Either way, I can't wait to meet her!' Oliver smiled, he couldn't wait to hold his tiny niece or nephew in his arms.

'I'll be its favourite,' Sophia joked.

'You will Soph! No offence Ol,' Lucy had teased Oliver, like back in their school days.

He'd smirked as he sipped on a glass of champagne.

'We'll see,' he joked back, as a layer of darkness clouded over his eyes.

***

Sophia smiled as she pushed herself further into the sofa. They were all so close.

CHAPTER TEN

December 16 2017, 8:00 a.m. Sophia and Oliver sat at the dining table in the kitchen wearing their pyjamas and matching, navy blue slippers, as they stared at the bowl of strawberries and blueberries, and a mug of green tea that sat between them. The sun shone through the window and into the kitchen, teasing them as it faded in and out through the clouds, beaming sunlight into the room one minute and then leaving them in the dimness of the shade the next.

The air was cold and bitter inside just as much as it was outside. Neither the heating nor the fireplace had been turned on and the atmosphere remained just as unpleasant and unfriendly as Sophia's nightmares.

But that didn't matter. Today marked the seventeen year anniversary of when Sophia and Oliver initially started dating, back in their final year of sixth form. Each year, for the last seventeen years, they would take a day off work to celebrate by doing something that they'd never done before. Oliver had been adamant that his cancer would return and spent his days setting Sophia up for when he would no longer be around.

Sophia sat at the table. Neither of them spoke. She closed her eyes as the sunlight beamed in through the window, shining directly onto her face.

'Happy anniversary,' she whispered beneath. He ignored her, his eyes still glaring into his mug of green tea that he now cradled in his hands.

She closed her eyes, avoiding the invisible tension that was forming between them.

***

Sophia lay beside Oliver on the sofa of her mums' living room. It was a cold and rainy Sunday evening and they'd just finished watching *Blood Brothers*, a short and tragic film about two life-long friends who were forced to walk down two different paths. It was a film that had been produced by one of Sophia's old friends from her previous town. Despite having lost contact with Cynthia, Cynthia remained one of the most loved and most inspirational people to have entered her life.

From a young age, Sophia needed approval from everyone around her. She helped others and made people smile putting her own needs aside to fulfil the ones of those around her. She was never able to ask for help, and never able to show she had any other emotion other than the happiness behind the fakeness of her smiles. During the day, she'd shy away, hiding her true feelings towards her life and some of the people within it and only at night, when winding down from the day, she would cry herself to sleep listening to the voices inside her head that reminded her that this life was never meant to be about her own happiness. There were too many people in the world with the ability to do her wrong just because she was weak.

Sophia had known Cynthia for just a year but she somehow managed to inspire Sophia's way of thinking, making her see that there was more to life than pleasing others. She'd given her random pep talks and opened her eyes to a new world that she wasn't ready to live in. Oliver's conversations would sometimes remind her of the strength and positivity that Cynthia had once shown her, but it was Oliver who had given it to her. It was Oliver who made her ready for that world, who held her hand while he pushed her along.

The credits to the film were coming to a close. Sophia blinked her eyes to stop the tears from forming following the unexpected death of one of the characters in the film. Oliver sat still, silenced by the tragedy.

'You ever thought about going back? Your old town? Cynthia?' Oliver asked as he placed his hand gently on Sophia's head.

'What shall we do to celebrate our first year Ol?' Sophia exchanged Oliver's questions with one of her own, shifting her thoughts to something more positive. Going back to her old town meant going back to the place that took her dad, the place that took a part of her soul and left her broken. Going back was something that Sophia would never be mentally prepared for.

Oliver smiled and stroked her hair. He understood.

'Whatever you want,' he'd said after a short pause.

'Dinner somewhere nice? A trip to the theatre? I heard *The Lion King* is meant to be really good.' She paused for Oliver to respond. Nothing.

'Maybe a nice weekend getaway? A picnic?' She continued as her body tightened up with nerves of being ignored. Their conversation may have moved on but her thoughts were with her old town, her dad, with Cynthia.

'No wait, it'll be cold.' Sophia looked down and sighed. 'I don't know,' she whispered, disappointed at herself for not knowing the words that Oliver wanted to hear.

Oliver continued to stroke her hair while Sophia closed her eyes, waiting for a response.

'That's all pretty standard isn't it? We can have dinner anytime, or a picnic, a weekend away, all of that. We can do that now if you want. What will we remember? What shall we do that we'll remember?'

Sophia began to feel nervous. Oliver had clearly been thinking about this for a while.

'What will be good for us, a positive experience that we will enjoy, one that will help us both?' Oliver paused and let his words sink in.

Sophia froze without any other reaction. She knew Oliver's thought process, and she knew she wasn't going to like what he had in mind.

'How about a bungee jump?' Oliver looked down slightly pushing Sophia away so he could see her face. There was something he found satisfying in watching the fear grow in her eyes.

'You must be joking!' Sophia reacted within a split second of Oliver's suggestion, moving even further away from him so he could see her face clearly at how uncomfortable she was with his proposal.

Oliver's lips spread across his face as his eyes began to glow through the darkness within them.

'Think about it Soph, it would…'

'Ol, I'm happy to stay home and make us a nice meal and you can come over and we can watch another DVD or something.' Sophia's words came flying out of her mouth at high speed, cutting off Oliver from speaking even more nonsense. He looked at her as she spoke, as she interrupted him.

'Soph, it's important to push yourself. Move outside of your little box now and again and push yourself to do something new…'

Sophia closed her eyes and turned her head away from his. She was agitated. He continued regardless.

'Try something you would never see yourself doing. Imagine how you would feel after a bungee jump, imagine if you like it?' Oliver pulled her back towards him, eyes still shadowed by the layer of darkness. She was still stiff but gave in to resting her body against his. He continued to stroke her hair.

Oliver had a strong belief in self-improvement and became fixated on pushing himself out of his comfort zone, trying to ensure that Sophia would do the same.

'Soph?'

She lay against his chest with her eyes closed, trying to avoid the situation, blocking it out. Oliver leaned in and kissed her forehead.

'Soph?' he whispered as he blew on her face, waiting for a reaction.

'No Ol,' Sophia spoke gently now. 'I can tell you now, I won't like it. I don't even like the thought of it. No Oli, if you want to do it, I promise, I'd support you but count me out. I'm happy to stay home and cook, for all of our anniversaries.' She looked away, annoyed at Oliver for having such a stupid suggestion for their first anniversary.

Oliver continued to stroke her hair.

'Okay, if not a bungee jump, how about a different experience, something else that we wouldn't usually do?' He paused. He didn't sense a reaction from Sophia. She was still tense, and her eyes had now been fixated on the corner of the coffee table. She didn't move.

'That way it will be new for both of us,' he moved his head closer to hers and kissed her forehead again before moving back into the sofa.

Sophia continued to stare at the corner of the coffee table, motionless and in silence.

'You need to be strong Soph. I may not always be here. Anything could happen and I don't want you to be here on our anniversary ten or twenty years' time and you're alone making a meal and eating it on your own. I don't want you to feel alone and scared for the rest of your life,' he sat back, knowing he'd won.

Sophia didn't move. Oliver continued.

'If we promise to do something positive, something we can both do together right now, it would be amazing. In ten years' time we could look back at all of the 'crazy' things we did and when it comes to us being old and grey, that's when we can stay home and cook. But right now, let's live. Live to the fullest. Let's celebrate each anniversary by doing something new.' Oliver moved his face back down again, pulling her closer to him, moving her face to his. 'Maybe not a bungee jump this time around, but that will definitely be something for the future. Build yourself up and see how much we can accomplish in the time we would have had dinner together, or gone on a weekend away. Let's live Soph. You know what life is to me. We can't waste it. Mine or yours,' he placed his hand on top of hers and rubbed it gently.

Sophia hesitated, slightly annoyed that Oliver had used his illness to get her to agree to something she was never going to be comfortable with. She was annoyed that she would have to try new things that took her out of her comfort zone for every anniversary, annoyed that she was never allowed to make her own decisions.

'Fine,' she relaxed her body pushing her head further into his chest. 'But you're never going to leave me,' she whispered, as she turned her hand to hold his.

He won.

***

Seventeen years later and here they were, at the kitchen table silently reminiscing about the past.

The sound of the phone ringing pulled Sophia out of her daydream. She looked at Oliver who was now sat with his head leaning on his arms, looking down at his mug of green tea.

'Hi, sorry we're not here to take your call right now…' the sound of Sophia's voice on the answering machine filled the room.

'But please leave a message after the beep and we'll get back to you when we can,' followed by Oliver's.

'Hi, I hope you're okay and keeping warm. The weather is changing fast, isn't it?' A familiar voice echoed through the speakers of the answering machine. The voice was soft and gentle. It was Isabella.

'I spoke to Lucy yesterday. She's very late so they will be inducing her today I believe. Bless her, she is scared but Tristan is a good boy, and his mum is supporting her too. I may go to see her. Maybe…'

The sound of her mums' voice made Sophia miss her instantly as the kindness and sweetness of her soul bounced into the room through the answering machine. Sophia automatically felt the warmth of her mother's love wrap around her.

'Maybe, you could come with me, what do you think?' Isabella's tone had dropped slightly and her voice became more hesitant, unsure of whether asking for company to see the new arrival was the right thing to do.

Despite trying to sound cheerful and happy, Sophia sensed sadness in Isabella's voice. If anyone knew Isabella's true feelings from just the sound of her voice, it was Sophia. The thought of her mum being down even the slightest, instantly made Sophia feel the sadness too.

'Anyway, I'm just calling to let you know that I am going to pop by this afternoon. I have something you may like, I'm sure you will like it. Please don't leave me standing out in the cold, I hear it will be raining later too. They're expecting snow but I don't know how much of that I believe, I sure hope not.' She stopped talking for a moment, letting silence fill the gap as she staggered with her next set of words. 'They're still asking questions. Have they come to you?' Isabella paused again, unsure of what else she could say. 'So, I'll see you later then,' she hesitated. 'I, I'll bring biscuits.' Isabella hung up.

Both Sophia and Oliver sat at the kitchen table. They'd both been listening to the message in silence, ignoring it and not showing any sign of acknowledging that their two life-long friends were soon to become parents, or that Isabella would soon be knocking on their front door, or that *they* were still asking questions.

The atmosphere in the kitchen had changed. The air had become colder and the distance between Sophia and Oliver grew in a matter of seconds. It seemed as if the walls and ceiling were starting to close in, suffocating Sophia and making her feel uncomfortable. The voices inside her head began to scream at her, reciting the lines from Oliver's book as the sounds scraped against the insides of her brain, like a trapped rat, desperately clawing its way out.

'Accidents happen, and that's exactly what it will be, an accident.' Her hands began to get clammy as she sat there watching Oliver who was still oblivious to what was going on. His head was still buried in his hands. Not knowing any other way to deal with the situation, Sophia excused herself from the dining table and left the kitchen, as though Oliver wasn't there and as if she'd never heard the message in the first place. But she did, and it replayed in her mind over and over.

She knew why her mum wanted to visit and she knew what her mum was going to say. Sophia refused to have to feel obliged to listen to Isabella just because she was her mum, and she hoped that Oliver felt the same way. She wasn't ready to accept the truth even if her mum was. She understood that one day she may have to give in and come to terms with the reality, but today wasn't that day, today was their seventeen year anniversary.

The voices in Sophia's head began to hiss all at once, uncomfortably as if each of them had unleased the demons inside their own souls. She didn't understand any of them as they hissed at her, holding her under water, depriving her of air. She needed to get away, to clear her mind and her thoughts, enough to be able to breathe, to hear what the voices were telling her. But she didn't want to listen. Maybe she was better off if she let them drown her. She wasn't sure. She put on her wooly, black winter coat and boots and left the house, leaving Oliver alone at the table.

It was just after 8:30 a.m. Sophia had already been on her early morning escape and hadn't intended to go for a run. Instead, she wanted to walk and fill her mind with happy thoughts. It was their seventeen year anniversary and it was going to be a positive one, despite the secrets and lies that surrounded her.

The street was busy with people on their way to work, kids being dropped off to school, and a few late joggers and dog walkers. Sophia walked slowly, taking in all of her surroundings. The sun was shining but failed to spread any warmth. It was cold and windy. The air was crisp and the trees were naked and bare, free from any leaves or any sign of life.

A little girl was running towards Sophia as she tried to catch up with her mum's longer strides.

Sophia moved out of her way and smiled at the little girl, thinking back to when she was forced to do the same when she used to walk to school with her dad. The girl didn't smile back. Sophia kept strolling, slowly towards the park, smiling at the little children, in their overly large hats, wrapped up in their scarves and coats.

Like the roads, the park was also busier than usual. The older and retired had come out for their morning walks, the late dog walkers, parents detouring through the park and walking home after dropping their children to school, and others taking their babies for a stroll in their pushchairs. Not too far from the park entrance were a group of ladies practising yoga – something Sophia had wished she'd taken up.

Sophia didn't move any further into the park, she stayed at the bench, away from the pond with the fountain. Regardless of feeling stronger today, she still feared for her most recent nightmare to come true. She sat at the bench and let time pass her by, listening to conversations of those who walked past her, seeing their happy faces, stress free and with all the time in the world. It was nice. The air was cold and fresh, and everything was bright despite it being a gloomy winter.

She sat back and smiled at herself as she closed her eyes picturing Oliver and herself as an old couple, walking together through the naked trees, around the park and stopping by at Lilly's for coffee. She sat there, hoping Oliver would join her. He didn't.

Hours had passed and Sophia hadn't moved from the bench. She listened to conversations between old couples and old friends, about baking biscuits when they got home, how they would be having their grandchildren over for the Christmas break and how beautiful the trees looked without their leaves.

She watched little children running around, laughing and being care free having only recently discovered how to use their little legs. She watched as people walked and talked to their dogs, waiting around for them patiently as the dogs ran free and innocently in and out of the trees, to their owners and back through the trees again. Sophia felt content and at peace, as she watched other people laughing and smiling. She watched as she realised there was a reason why these people looked so happy. There was one thing they all had in common. They made time. All of these people took the time to appreciate the smaller things in life, the things that were easily ignored and overlooked as adults growing up. They made time to be around nature and actually enjoy it. Regardless of the weather, regardless of having other duties in life, they made time in their day to get out into the park and walk, peacefully without getting lured into the busy and rushed lifestyle that went on outside of the park gates.

She wished she'd appreciated her surroundings more and gave more time to the good things in life itself. She wished she'd taken more time out with Oliver, to sit and value everything around them, everything that had been on their doorstep for so many years but had been abandoned due to other priorities and DVD nights.

She closed her eyes, thinking of all of their anniversaries and everything they did do, moving the focus away from the things they didn't do.

***

'Okay, so, if not the bungee jump this year, how about we conquer your fear of heights to prepare you for that?' Oliver asked.

'Prepare me for that? What's *that*?' Sophia was confused and becoming frustrated again. 'I thought an anniversary was a couple thing, this is supposed to be our thing. Prepare me for what Oli, when has our anniversary become just my thing?'

Oliver ignored Sophia's frustration again.

'There's that place near Green Hill Park, where you can do the treetop walk. Tristan and Lucy did it a few months ago, shall we do that?'

Sophia had gone silent, and turned her head towards the window, watching as the raindrops raced down the glass.

'I wonder, is it normal for couples to not look forward to an anniversary? Here I was thinking an anniversary was a celebration of romance and love or something, for us to have some fun and spend more time together doing nice things. But no, we're going to be doing things I hate. Aren't I lucky?' she said sarcastically, still annoyed.

Oliver said nothing. He smiled as he waited for her to continue. She didn't.

'Okay Soph, how about a nice getaway for a few days like you said.' Oliver paused. Sophia waited, she knew there was more to it. 'And you drive.' There it was. 'Anywhere over three hours away. Actually, we split the drive, so you do the first half, and I do the second. How does that sound?'

'I can't drive for that long.' She didn't hesitate to push back.

'It will be nice, a nice getaway, trust me on this. If at any point you feel overwhelmed, I will be there. You have to push yourself.'

Sophia smiled uncomfortably, knowing he wasn't going to let her win. He was stubborn, and she was weak, but as much as she hated confrontation, this was one battle she wasn't going to back down on.

She turned up to look at Oliver. His eyes glistened and sparkled with so much beauty as he looked back at her.

'Fine,' she agreed.

Of all of her weaknesses, Oliver was her biggest.

***

Sophia opened her eyes. She felt so much more at peace, looking back at their years together, at all of the things she'd accomplished in those years thanks to Oliver.

They'd gone away to Devon for a few days and had stayed at a hotel in a small town in Torquay. They'd shared the drive as Oliver had suggested. It was the furthest she'd ever driven, and the first time driving out of her town. She was scared and nervous, but she did it regardless.

After that, she'd begun to drive more comfortably for longer distances. They'd gone away to the Cotswolds too and she'd driven there and back along the narrow roads. She hated every minute of it but felt good about it afterwards. Having Oliver there beside her gave her the push she needed to realise that she was the only one stopping herself from being able to be free. Driving was just one of the many things she believed she wasn't able to do, but managed to do so with Oliver's encouragement and belief.

'Next year we can go to Green Hill Park,' she said on their drive back from Devon.

Oliver smiled. 'Then the bungee?' he asked cheekily. Sophia ignored him and continued to drive.

On their second anniversary, they walked the tree tops at Green Hill Park, despite it being freezing cold. For their third, they stayed out in a tent in the dimly lit park overnight to wait to see the sunrise. On their fourth anniversary, Oliver pushed Sophia to do a presentation to a small group of local charity owners, pitching a business idea to help raise funds through her paintings which started off her side career as an artist. Their fifth was a holiday away, with all decisions, planning and organising carried out by Sophia, something she would never have seen herself doing on her own. On their sixth year, Sophia took it upon herself to surprise Oliver. She had tracked down the family home of Oscar, and they drove down to Brighton to visit him. It wasn't until their seventh year when they finally joined the London 170ft Bungee Jump as part of a charity fundraiser, raising a total of £1,612 between them. For their eighth year anniversary, they went camping for three days, living out in a tent, learning to make a fire and living on canned food. Oliver proposed to Sophia on their ninth year anniversary and they married the following year in autumn 2010. They spent their time after that saving up and working to pay off their mortgage and working towards fulfilling their personal goals. Despite their yearly anniversary challenges becoming smaller because of it, they never failed to spend it together and were content and grateful to be able to focus on the things they wanted to do.

It was these experiences Sophia would leave out on the surface, hiding the torture that she went through to complete them. Ignoring the sacrifices she made to win Oliver's love.

Today, on their seventeenth anniversary, whilst sitting on her own on this park bench, Sophia decided it was time to face her biggest fear – the fear of being scared. This year, she was going to stop running away.

Her most recent nightmare and recollections of the past left her feeling as though she had no choice but to be ready to accept her fate. She knew she'd soon learn from her nightmares, whatever they were trying to say. It was clear the time was coming, and despite not being ready, she continuously told herself she was, until she could begin to believe it.

Hours had passed and Sophia was still sitting at the bench. The ladies practising yoga had departed, the mums and their babies had vanished and just a few dog walkers were left. An old man who had been walking around the park with his dog came and sat beside Sophia on the bench. His dog ran around the bench, further out to the trees and back to the bench again. The man lit up a cigarette and inhaled as he watched his dog run back and forth. He didn't look at Sophia or make any threatening gesture towards her but within seconds of her feeling brave and content, her meerkat like instinct of running away flooded her thoughts and she decided she'd been in the park long enough.

She left the park having already failed her newly self-assigned anniversary challenge. But there was still time to start again.

CHAPTER ELEVEN

Sophia took the usual route home, past her old high school, the petrol station and the blocks of houses. A feeling of calmness and contentment surrounded her, even more so when she began to pass the local church. A strong and invisible force stopped her in her path, pulling her towards the church, luring her in. The voices inside her head began to make ghastly sounds, as they slithered around inside her mind, jumbling up what was real and what was not.

The church had been there ever since she'd moved into the area but she had never felt so enticed to go in, despite how much of a landmark it was in the area, and knowing how much it would have meant to both Oliver and Tristan. Sophia lost faith after her dad had passed, although she and Oliver did want to visit together, to say 'thank you' and pray for their happiness together.

A sudden feeling of guilt arose in her throat from deep within her gut. Something was inviting her in, and whether she wanted to or not, she was going to obey it, even if it was without Oliver.

As she turned towards the church, warmth touched her body. She saw it as a sign, a positive one, and the next challenge that she needed to fulfil. She was going in.

She walked through the church gates, slowly along a steep, hilly path. Tombstones were upright on each side, some with fresh flowers placed beside them, some without. Some had been kept well whilst others had looked as though they hadn't been visited in a long time. In some areas, stones had eroded, along with the words that had been carved among them, shrubbery and weeds took back their right to grow over the land and around the gravestones and the cages of some had become rusty.

Sophia looked down, not wanting to stare and disrespect those that were no more. She walked on until she came up to the entrance to the church.

It was remarkable. The church had originally been built over nine hundred years ago, and although it had been restored, it still remained just as picturesque as it did when it was first built, if not more now with its ruinous and historic white stone.

A large steeple protruded from the top of the building, topped by a famous spire which was covered with twelve tons of lead and could be seen from miles away, making it one of the most popular and recognisable landmarks in the area.

Two large brown wooden doors with extraordinary hand-carvings of angels were pushed open to the sides. Sophia explored the artwork in amazement as she walked through into a large porch like area of the church entrance, touching the carvings and running her fingers across the rusty gold of the large door handles. The words 'A place of peace and a prayer for all people' were carved across the doors, welcoming in anyone, religious or not. Her eyes followed the pattern from the top of the door all the way down to the ground until she noticed the patterns on the floor beneath her. Small blue, white and green mosaic tiles filled the floor, positioned together to create images of various birds and flowers.

Sophia couldn't believe all the detail and passion behind what she was seeing, the beauty and art that had been on her doorstep all these years, everything that she had walked past without acknowledging any of it. She wondered if there was more around her that she'd failed to notice. She had never imagined a church to be so beautiful.

She entered the church being invited in by the beauty of the exterior. It wasn't as dark as she imaged it to be. Light came beaming in through the colourful clerestory windows which framed by carved marble arches. She walked in, continuing to admire the beauty in the paintings of angels, long bearded men and naked women that were on the walls from the ground all the way up to the ceiling. Arches and pillars stood on both sides and were decorated and carved similarly to that of the large door at the entrance to the building. She continued to walk through the nave of the church in amazement as she took in the beauty of 377 carvings along the roofs of the nave and transepts, which were said to be some of the finest in the county.

It was quiet but unlike the silence in her nightmares, the atmosphere in the church failed to carry the same sense of fear. This was peaceful, and although near enough empty, Sophia instantly felt safe, warm and free.

She walked towards the altar at front of the church. A large cross was erected in the centre, with three fine arches framing three tall and narrow lancet windows with more patterns of angels behind. The area was raised slightly and was blanketed with a red and gold carpet. The rest of the space was empty. A large brass organ had been placed at the south side of the chancel. So much beauty and care was held within the churches architecture and interior. Sophia was astounded at how she had overlooked the magnificence within something so close to her home, slightly embarrassed at the same time, at how she was able to believe that such a beautiful place would be too disturbing for her to visit.

She stood at the foot of the chancel and without realising, closed her eyes tightly as she put her hands together in prayer for the first time in over twenty four years. She prayed, with hope, in desperation.

'I don't know what I'm doing, or what brings me to you,' Sophia shivered as a chill ran down her spine. She kept her eyes closed tightly, tensing up her shoulders as she continued to pray, desperate like a little girl who has been told her father is no more. She prayed, opening up her heart in front of God, showing him her scars as they revealed her weakness, as they revealed her strength. Imaginary dust of peace and love sprinkled over her. Silent music played inside her head as she began to relax, floating like a bubble, soft and gentle. The steady drum of her heartbeat added to the melody as she began to feel lighter than the transient round mirrors around her as they reflected swirls of rainbow streams, glistening and shimmering as they drifted gently, dancing to the harmonic sounds inside her head.

Sophia opened her eyes, staring straight at the man on the cross. Her bubble had popped.

'I need you to take care of Oliver.' She blurted out, alarmed, as she frightened herself with her own voice as it bounced against the walls and back into her ears. No-one was there. She continued, this time in a whisper. 'I need him to be happy and follow his dreams. This pain, this emptiness, I will feel it for as long as it takes, but I need Oliver to be okay.'

She went down to her knees and bowed her head. 'Please free his mind from his past, free his pain and let him be at peace.' She prayed hard, in desperation, as her thoughts and feelings evaporated from her soul and into the man on the cross. She remained that way, desperate, for almost over an hour.

The church had become darker as thick clouds closed in outside, obstructing the light from entering the building. The murmurs of a young couple sliced through Sophia's prayers as they walked into the church. Sophia, who had now opened her eyes, jumped up onto her feet, in fear and ready to run if she needed to.

Remorse ran through her body as she saw the young couple walk through the church. She and Oliver had said they would go to the church and pray together but they never made time, something had always come up and prayer had become less of a priority. Sophia looked down, ashamed that it had taken her so long. She was ashamed at the excuses she had made for not going, and for having waited so long. She wondered whether things would have turned out differently had she gone to visit sooner. She closed her eyes and wondered, praying with regret, whether this was her karma for not going. She wondered whether God had been punishing her, whether He intended for the bad to happen as a way of bringing her to Him.

She turned and walked past the couple as they entered the church, looking down to avoid any eye contact. It should have been her and Oliver.

She left through the large wooden doors, into the graveyard and outside the church gates, wishing she had made time. Maybe then, things would be different.

It was nearly 2:00 p.m. now and Sophia had spent all morning trying to appreciate and value time and her surroundings, wishing she'd made more time with Oliver, for them both to have done it together. Regardless of how she felt when she'd left the church, Sophia still had a feeling of contentment which remained within her. She felt like she'd accomplished something today, something she'd been afraid of for so many years. Today, Sophia felt as though she was becoming closer, closer than she had ever been, to facing her biggest fear of accepting her fate. She wasn't ready to go home.

Sophia had been walking for nearly twenty minutes. She'd taken detours around her local area, discovering places she'd never seen before, enjoying the views, turning into the roads with large trees that arched over the streets, walking through the tunnels and seeing even more beauty on the other side. She wondered whether she had been there before, and wished she'd walked down this side of the town more often. She imagined the streets in autumn, when the grounds would be carpeted with red and gold leaves. She embraced the beauty of nature. Even now, in the cold, dull atmosphere.

Sophia kept on walking, taking in the sights around her. She bounced from cloud to cloud, happily. Even the voices inside her head were joyful as they pulled on the harmonic strings within her soul, producing a serene melody that played in the background of her thoughts like a soundtrack to her film, and she was the star. She felt light as she floated along the footpath, admiring all the good in life. She was in heaven.

It was reaching nearly 2:45 p.m. and the clouds had become darker. The atmosphere became still as the thick and heavy clouds stretched across the sky. The street became gloomy, birds flew quickly to shelter themselves from the showers that were soon to come, and the sign of any human life disappeared as people scurried from the streets and into their homes. The sky grumbled as the sound of thunder in the distance moved through the air, cutting through the harmonic strings from within her.

There wasn't long to go now until the skies were to open, releasing the buckets of rain that it had been preparing to wash away the evil, cleansing the earth and everyone within it.

Sophia had turned back. The thick, dark clouds were coming closer, and the skies were becoming angrier as the thunder roared louder and louder. Everything looked different in the shadows, less magical and unwelcoming. She increased her pace to get home faster. The voices inside her head had been muttering quietly, but she didn't know what they were saying. She just knew she needed to get home.

The street was dead and eerie. Sophia felt strange. Her gut clenched. Numbness began to spread through her veins. There was something unnerving about her surroundings. She was unsure, not knowing if this was her paranoia kicking in, or a warning. How could you tell? Something wasn't right. The feeling of sickness hovered around her throat. She kept swallowing her own saliva, trying not to vomit as the knot in her gut tightened further. The voices continued to taunt at her but she couldn't make out the words through the sounds. Her eyes felt heavy, compressed by a sudden weight that sat over her. Her insides began to sizzle. Her forehead was sticky with sweat. A surge of exhaustion struck her body. She was tired. Sophia continued to walk, dragging her feet along the pavement, trying to focus on getting home.

The voices inside her head began to murmur louder, muffled. She knew it was a warning, but still didn't know what they were saying. She slowed down, wary as she got closer to her house. She could see it from a distance, but something was off. She began to move closer to the road, paranoid that someone was lurking within the bushes, alley ways or in the front gardens of the other houses, waiting for her. She walked in the middle of the road, exposed, with nothing to hide behind.

She wondered how she had allowed her imagination to get this far. She wondered if, like her nightmares, she had been making up her reality. She didn't know what existed and what didn't, were the voices inside her head really there? Was there anyone there to run from? She focused on the house and kept moving forward, unsure of how real her life was.

'I'm not crazy.' She whispered underneath her breath. She stopped dead in her tracks.

Sophia watched as she stood, stationary in the middle of the road. She watched as a shadow moved outside her front door. She watched as it stood there, waiting. She watched. The confirmation that none of it was her imagination charged through her. It was real. Her voices, her instincts, her feelings. It was all real. She watched, as this figure stood there, waiting at the top of the steps, outside her home, waiting for her.

CHAPTER **TWELVE**

The dark ominous figure stood outside her front door. Sophia's eyes were fixated on it. She watched it, moving, swaying, lurking outside her house. Questions after questions burst through her head. The answers were there, ahead of her, outside her front door. All she had to do was let her feet follow the road. But she was scared, gutless, in denial.

The figure moved closer to the front door, banging his fist against the damp wood. Sophia closed her eyes instantly, as the memory of the first time she was approached by the man with the blurred face came flooding back. It was the first of her many nightmares, when he came knocking on her front door while she had been asleep. The loud, toxic sound of banging and thudding, hammered through her ears in the middle of the night, waking up only Sophia.

'Oliver,' she panicked. Sophia began to walk towards her house, wishing for Oliver not to open the door. She began to speed up. She had to protect him. She continued to walk, faster, wishing she'd told him, even warned him, about the man with the blurred face and about everything else that had been going on inside her head. She began to run, ready to face her truth. This was it. She was ready to face it. At least then, her nightmare would be over.

She ran, with her eyes still fixated on the figure that was waiting outside her front door. She would approach him from behind, he'd least expect it. He was standing there, at her front door, with his back to her, waiting for her to let him in. Sophia slowed down, allowing herself more time to plan out how she was going to capture this man. He would not have been expecting her to approach him from behind. She had the upper hand. Today, she would defeat this man, today she would get her answers, and today the nightmares and torture will be over. She looked up. Strong and on a mission, like a lion who'd escaped from its cage.

'Please Ol, don't answer the door,' she whispered as she continued to tread down the road, thinking about her next move. The sound of thunder rumbled through the air again, this time a lot louder and a lot angrier. Sophia stopped.

Deep inside, underneath her mask, she was still afraid. She stopped in the middle of the road, not too far from her house now, wondering why the man with the blurred face was knocking on her front door. She flashed back to the moment she saw him at the park sitting on the bench, and again in the car park standing outside her passenger door. Her heart started to beat faster as she realised he would have already known she wasn't home. After all this time, even when he was behind her, chasing her, he was always one step ahead.

The clouds became thicker and darker creating a shadow of black onto the street. The rain began to fall from the sky making it even harder for Sophia to make out this figure that was standing outside her front door. She began to move forwards, towards this figure, hoping Oliver wasn't home to answer. She walked slowly, attempting for the first time, to look at his face, trying to make out who it could be.

The voices inside her head began to scream as her heart raced faster than lightening, causing sparks of electricity to run through her body, jump-starting like a dead car bought back to life. But despite being charged, her fuel ran low as it began to leak through her veins, faster with each step she took as she came closer to the house, to the figure. She was there standing in a pool of gasoline, at the bottom of the steps, looking directly at the figure.

The figure stood there, facing the door, waiting. It wasn't the man with the blurred face. The figure was much shorter and slimmer. Sophia walked up the steps. Isabella was standing at the door waiting to be let in. Sophia sighed. Relieved, but disappointed.

Isabella wore a long creamy, brown coat, with a baby pink Burberry scarf, black trousers and flat brown boots. Like Sophia, Isabella always dressed immaculately. But despite her efforts in her outfit, Isabella looked different. She always had a small frame but Sophia could see she had lost a lot of weight over the past few months. She looked small and fragile and her hair had become thin and lifeless. Her face had become shrunken, pale and wrinkly, and her lips had lost their fullness. She had aged drastically.

Sophia greeted her mum with a smile as she tried to be strong and hold back the tears. As grateful as she was to finally be seeing her mum after so long, seeing her look so fragile and weak made Sophia feel just the same. Of all of the changes in her appearance, Isabella's eyes had changed the most. They were filled with sadness and pain, with no life or feeling other than unhappiness and emptiness inside them. It was evident, that she was also suffering from sleepless nights. Sophia had seen this pain in her mums eyes once before.

Tears of guilt began to fill Sophia's eyes at the thought of her mum suffering alone, not eating, sleeping, or not having anyone to talk to.

'Don't!' A voice from inside her head roared at her. She wiped her tears away quickly. Isabella didn't need to see Sophia cry. Today, she was strong.

Oliver had finally opened the door. Isabella walked into the house and Sophia followed behind, both taking off their boots before walking through to the living room. Oliver closed the front door and walked through behind them.

'Sorry, I was in the shower. I hope you weren't waiting out there long.' Oliver lied. He'd been sitting at the bottom of the steps, wondering whether or not he needed Isabella's company, and Sophia knew it.

Sophia and Isabella had now been seated on the sofa, no words exchanged between them. Isabella looked around, as if seeing the room for the first time.

'How nice. It is nice and cosy in here isn't it? I see you've been keeping it as spotless as ever.' Isabella ignored the pile of papers on the table, and the half empty mug of cold, green tea without a coaster. She ignored the unfolded blanket shoved in the corner of the sofa, and the open, empty DVD cases of *Stand By Me* and *The Green Mile* that sat on the coffee table. She also ignored the empty mug and fruit bowl that sat on the smaller table beside the sofa, and the fact that the curtains were still closed.

'Maybe we could put the fire on?' She crossed her arms and rubbed her elbows. 'Here, let me.' Isabella got up from the sofa and made her way to the fireplace.

Sophia would usually have the fire on whenever she was home, especially when she knew her mum would be coming over. She would make sure the house was nice and warm regardless of what season it was. Isabella was always cold. If ever the fire wasn't on, it would be the first thing Isabella would do upon entering their home.

Sophia and Oliver always made sure that Isabella was comfortable enough to treat their home as if it was her own. They wanted her to feel as welcome in their home as she made them feel in hers, and Oliver would always remind her that it was her home as much as it was Sophia's and his, and that she was always welcome, whatever time of day, although he didn't always answer the door. He was good with words.

Oliver sat and watched as Isabella filled the room with a glowing tint of gold and orange creating a feeling of warmth and peace, as she always did.

'Now, that's better isn't it?' Isabella walked towards the window and opened the curtains, letting in the tiny bit of light from the lamppost outside, before taking a seat back on the sofa, rubbing her hands together at the same time. She kept her coat on and made herself comfortable. 'Ahh, yes. That's much better.' Isabella wrapped the fluffy grey blanket around her legs the same the way that Sophia would.

They listened to the crackling sounds of the burning firewood.

'I hope you're keeping well,' Isabella looked around as she spoke. 'I hope...'

The sound of the house phone ringing interrupted Isabella and she stopped, feeling slightly relieved from having to make the initial small talk. It was a struggle.

The phone continued to ring and she watched as

no-one moved to answer it. She felt the awkwardness of knowing well that phone calls were no longer being answered in this household. She'd been on the receiving end of being ignored many times and it was always unnerving. Even during the times when she'd call with the intention of leaving a message on the answering machine, she was still left feeling disappointed when no-one picked up her call.

Everyone paused in silence.

'Aren't you going to get that?' Isabella looked at the phone, knowing that neither her question nor the phone, were going to be answered. She felt embarrassed as she pictured the many times she would call and had nothing in return.

No-one said anything as they waited for the ringing to stop. Sophia's voice took over on the machine.

'Hi, sorry we're not here to take your call right now…'

'But please leave a message after the beep and we'll get back to you when we can,' Oliver's voice followed.

There was a slight pause after the beep and Isabella moved to stand up as though she was going to pick up the phone. A voice came through the machine, muffled as though there was a distance between the caller and their phone.

'I don't think it beeped, I didn't hear it…' It was Tristan.

'Let me see…' Lucy's voice followed in the

background. She sounded different. She sounded drained and tired, lifeless. 'It's fine, poor connection probably, but I think it's there. Hello? Must be recording,' she continued.

They listened to the sound of banging and interruption through the machine as Lucy passed the phone back to Tristan.

'Hello? Heyyyy! Not sure if you can hear me. Pick up if you can.' Tristan's voice was loud and strong and carried cheer and enjoyment as it bounced off the walls. He paused, giving time for someone to answer his call. 'Okay, maybe not! But yeah, I'm officially a dad!' Tristan laughed out of excitement over the machine. Everyone in the room remained seated and silent. 'We had to tell you first. We just had a gorgeous baby, not even been an hour. God you should be here, this feels amazing, so tiny, like Vel, but luckily this little thing has my features,' he teased. 'We all look forward to seeing you! Vel sends her love.'

The sweet sounds of a tiny babies purr played in the background as Tristan continued.

'Come soon, seriously. Peace.' The sound of muffled banging mixed with the soft purrs filled the silence. Lucy's voice echoed in the distance but she wasn't close enough for anyone to make out what she was saying.

'Oh God, yeah,' Tristan held the phone to his ears again. 'So, guess what we've named this little beauty? Don't leave it too long. Peace.' Tristan hung up.

Isabella closed her eyes, looked up and exhaled deeply. She let herself smile briefly, before a tear rolled down her cheek and dripped from her chin and onto her lap. Oliver sat still, focusing on a small crack on the wall in front of him, frozen and numb.

Sophia watched Oliver and her mum for a few seconds, trying again to hold back her tears like her mother had once taught her. The sound of thunder outside beamed through the house and not too long after, the sounds of strong, heavy rain slamming against the window filled the room. The thick clouds covered any bit of light in the skies outside, but the room inside came to life by the dancing flames of the fire. The fire had created a beautiful ambience with its steady movement of light, the glowing oranges and golds subtly lighting up areas of the room, casting smooth shadows across the walls. The sound of wood burning inside as the rain poured against the windows outside created a sense of peace, but despite this, the atmosphere in the room became cold and empty.

Sophia glanced over at Oliver and Isabella again. Neither of them had moved from their initial stances. The voices inside her head began to murmur all at once. She hated how they had been behaving. She left the room, running up the stairs, and locking herself inside the bathroom. The sound of thunder filled her ears. She let herself cry loudly, she couldn't fight it. Despite her life lessons from Isabella, from Cynthia and from Oliver, Sophia was still weak. The voices were right. She was never going to be strong.

She stood in the bathroom, staring at her reflection in the mosaic mirror. Her face was soaked from the tears that were pouring from her eyes. All the signs were telling her it was time to face the truth, but her heart wanted to run away. She wasn't ready. She began to feel her insides tearing apart as everything started to become real.

The man with the blurred face wasn't there, she wasn't being chased or watched, she wasn't even stuck in a nightmare, yet she still found herself to be running away. She'd been drowning herself every day, forcing her head underwater, not realising she was a fish. There was no escape. Reality began to take effect as she realised that no matter what she did and where she went, she really had nowhere to hide. Her thoughts, the voices inside her head and everything that had haunted her throughout her whole life were loyal to her and were going to remain with her forever.

She heard the baby babbling in her ears as it replayed over and over, and the reality of the past nine months began to kick in.

'Life goes on,' she whispered as she stared into her soul through the mirror.

While Sophia had been holding on to the past, Tristan and Lucy had already had their baby. It was already winter. Nine months had gone by, and for her, nothing had changed. Her life had stopped, but time never did.

'Fear makes you stop. But time waits for no-one,'

she heard Oliver say to her, back when they were in sixth form, finally truly understanding what it meant. She broke down, realising she had all the answers to all of her questions. It was time.

She cried, releasing her demons, the voices and everything inside her as she prepared for herself to come to terms with the truth. She stared at herself in the mirror, seeing nothing but emptiness in her eyes. She washed her face, destroying the evidence of pain before heading into spare room, ignoring the fact that her mum was still downstairs. She lied to herself. She was still hiding, still running away, still not ready to face the truth.

Sophia sat on one of the boxes, looking around, unsure of what she wanted to find. Her body could run away, but her mind was always in the same place. Sophia was in need of something to distract her. She wasn't even close to being ready.

She walked towards the shelf and gently moved her fingers along the ornaments and other objects that carried some of the best memories of her life. Her fingers moved across a stack of books. One of them caught her eye. It was a small, A5 navy blue notebook with a picture of a yellow lion that sat at the bottom of the spine. She took out the book and ran her fingers along the cover which displayed a larger, 3D version of the lion.

Sophia flicked through the handwritten notes inside as the scent of Armani aftershave filled her nostrils. She closed her eyes and smiled as she embraced the warm sensation that now surrounded her. The snakes inside her began to move, slowly, as they wrapped around her gut, soothing her insides until suddenly, they squeezed tightly, sending sharp pains through her stomach, jolting her back to reality, away from her trance. She opened her eyes, still holding on to her notebook, tightly. Sophia continued to flick through the pages, and began to read random passages within it.

February 20th 2017

We went to Lilly's today, to work on a new business venture together. It's strange, while you were writing notes, I sat there watching you, thinking about us, and how both our paths just seem to 'fit'. It's so strange. I love seeing the passion in you, it keeps me going. It's pretty cool, not many people have what we do. I am grateful.

March 2nd 2017

Ecstatic. Lucy is pregnant which means we'll be an Uncle and Aunty soon. I'm so grateful after all these years, to still have such a close knit circle of friends. And now the family is expanding with their little one. One day we may even have our own. Who knows? This is a nice feeling.

Sophia smiled. Throughout the years, Sophia and Oliver had begun to write down their feelings and thoughts in a journal. Sometimes it was just a line or a small paragraph once or twice a week, or sometimes once a month, so they could one day look back and see their progression, and see how much their lives had improved and changed over time.

She closed her eyes and smiled as she thought back to the moment Oliver implemented this strange, new way of documenting their development.

***

The clock struck twelve and Sophia and Oliver had stayed up to watch the fireworks from across the world as they celebrated the start of 2001.

Oliver had handed a pack of journals over to Sophia, each with 360 blank pages inside. He had a pack for himself too.

'I read something on the internet the other day, off some website, some motivational thing about life.' He turned his body to face Sophia and moved hers to face him. 'Look at where we were, and where we are now. How did we get here Soph? It's easy to miss these things. One day you get to somewhere and you don't know yourself how you got there.'

Sophia listened to the passion in his words. His eyes sparkled and lit up and Sophia loved him that much more because of it.

Oliver reached into a gap in the sofa and pulled out the two different packs of journals.

'Here.' Oliver presented her with one of them. 'And here's one for me too. The lion and panda,' he smiled.

Sophia didn't know how to react. It was weird and not something she would usually do. She sat there still, focused on Oliver's face, his eyes. They were beautiful.

'Sometimes you have those moments where life seems still, bad things happen and you don't know where you're going and how you even got to where you are. This little log book can remind you, it all takes time. Some things take so much time you don't even know it's happening, but it is happening. Keeping a log book can make you see that. Each day is a step, each day is progress.'

Sophia had no words. The idea sounded cheesy but perfect at the same time. She loved how much he valued the things an ordinary person would ignore and take for granted. Like time, progression was also so important and so precious.

They had agreed it would be positive words only, things that made them feel happy, content and satisfied so when they were to look back, they would feel positive about their lives, focusing on just the good.

'I can do that,' Sophia said as she smiled and took a pack of books from Oliver.

Of all the things that Sophia was good at, pretending that evil and nastiness was non-existent was one of them. She could easily journal on the good things, burying all of the negativity deep within her mind.

Sophia smiled as she saw the fireworks light up

through Oliver's eyes, moving in to hug him and smelling the musky scent of his Armani aftershave.

***

She continued to read.

March 3rd 2017
We're going to Lake Como tomorrow. Not sure what else to say. Twenty four years. Life is amazing, but we need to pack so I can't write much. I'm just so grateful for this. Thank you God.

Oliver was right, looking back at the memories and reading this today made Sophia feel warm and happy. She didn't want it to end. She flicked through some of the pages and continued to read.

April 6th 2017
Denial and isolation, anger, bargaining, depression and acceptance. It's been a month and this is what I'm hearing. Where am I at this precise moment? Are these really the steps people face when dealing with loss? What have I lost? Everything. Does anyone ever really accept losing everything?

The warmth in her body and the smile on her face vanished. The feeling of happiness and positivity had left the book.

July 7th 2017

I watched the sunset yesterday, from the spare room. I could feel you with me and we watched it together until there was no light, other than the tiny glare from the street lamps, the ones you used to say weren't bright enough. You're right, they're not that bright.

July 10th 2017

Everything is a memory, and a good one. But I have to focus on my dreams. That's all we have left isn't it?

August 2nd 2017

It's so hard. None of this feels real. I wish things weren't the way they are, and I wish things didn't end up the way it has. What am I supposed to do? I know I have to go on, I can keep saying that until it happens, and just hope it happens. But my happiness? It's with you.

Sophia closed the journal, wishing she'd never looked at it. Her mind raced as the memories came flooding back in. Everything she'd been ignoring, everything she'd been running away from, all there in black and white. The truth.

Tears didn't roll from her eyes this time, the shock of what this was left her numb. She moved to the floor and closed her eyes as she lay there, in silence. Her heart-rate slowed and her face became pale as though every ounce of life was being sucked out of her. Her eyes no longer sparkled and, as if almost instantly, her hair had become as thin and lifeless as Isabella's. She took a deep breath before relaxing her body deep into the beige carpet as the reality of the past nine months began to kick in.

She lay there, silently running her fingers along the 3D picture of the lion on the cover, waiting for the strength to open it and read a little more. She needed to stop running and finally face the truth. And this little journal was the only thing that had all the answers to her questions.

The rain continued to fall outside, with the sound of every drop hitting the window echoing through the room and into Sophia's ears.

Ten minutes had passed and Sophia lay across the floor still running her fingers along the journal.

'The lion and panda,' she saw Oliver smile as he presented her with her pack. She smiled and closed her eyes for a few moments before opening them. She moved the journal closer to her, turning chunks of the pages towards the end to continue reading.

September 19th 2017
I watched Stand by Me, I couldn't watch it until the end. All the memories. Every memory and every thought, they eat away at me and I want to forget but I can't. I want to not care and I want to move on and carry on. I see the sunset, sometimes I even see it rise. I see the colours of the autumn leaves. I see everything, and I just want it to be us again. I know the world hasn't ended, I know my world hasn't ended.

I know the value of life and I appreciate it and value it. But some things aren't fair and other things just don't make any sense at all.

September 21st 2017
The days are bad but the nights are the hardest. That's when it all comes back and I have nothing to do to keep myself from thinking about you. I have to let it go. I have to let it all go. This isn't good for anyone. Not every ending is a happy one. I deserved this after all.

Sophia put the pages down. She recognised this pain too well. She needed to go downstairs and be with Oliver. She stood up and put the journal back on the shelf before heading out of the room and down the stairs. Once again, Sophia ignored the reality, pretending everything was okay, in denial behind the truth of what she'd read.

She walked into the living room. Oliver and Isabella were sitting on the larger sofa. Sophia made her way to the single one by the window. Isabella had her back to Sophia, facing Oliver who was still staring at the crack in the wall. Isabella stood up.

'I'll put the kettle on shall I? These homemade biscuits will go down nicely with a cup of tea.'

Isabella wasn't as strong as she made out to be. After losing her husband, she had gone through severe depression. She'd been in denial for such a long time, and had learnt how to numb her pain and hide it around Sophia. Night time was the worst, and she would release all of her agony by crying herself to sleep. Sophia would listen each night, to the sound of her mum's heart breaking over and over as she cried herself to sleep. Their pain was a secret they'd kept silently between themselves. A secret neither of them would ever speak of, not even to each other.

Isabella made her way into the kitchen. Sophia followed. Oliver stayed on the sofa, still staring at the crack in the wall, in deep thought and oblivious to what was happening around him.

Sophia watched her mum make tea. Isabella smiled happily and pretended she was relaxed and okay about everything as she put the kettle on, cleaning up as she went along. Sophia just watched, seeing for the first time, where she got it from. No words were exchanged between them, but they could both feel so much love regardless.

After a few minutes, they walked back into the living room. Isabella put down the tray on the table beside the smaller sofa by the window where Sophia had sat. This time she took a seat on the smaller sofa, giving Sophia the opportunity to sit beside Oliver, who was still numb and still staring at the crack in the wall.

Isabella picked up her bag and rummaged through it. She picked out a little frame from inside.

'I thought you may like this.' Isabella stood up and placed it on the coffee table facing both Sophia and Oliver. It was Sophia's vision board from years ago, when she still lived at home with Isabella. She'd kept it in her room beside her bedside table to see every morning and every night. Both Sophia and Oliver sat and studied the images within the frame. The frame had collage of various photos inside it, including one of seven smiley faces, a set of paint brushes, a book, a little house, and a photo of Sophia and Oliver. Sophia smiled. She hadn't seen the vision board in years. Oliver looked back at the wall and continued to stare at the crack within it.

'I assume you haven't spoken to anyone,' Isabella interrupted his focus. 'If we talk about it together it might help. It might help me too.' She tensed up for a moment before finally letting herself relax, relieved that she managed to say what she'd been wanting to say for hours. 'I'm here for you. You need to talk to someone, *we* need to talk to someone, to each other even,' she continued, knowing she would have nothing back in return. She was in the house, which was the closest she'd been in months, so that was a positive sign. 'Time is a healer, I can promise you that. It will get better. You will always remember the pain, and it will probably always be there, but life goes on remember? You can't give up.'

The atmosphere in the room began to change. From what felt like a mother's love now felt like the beginning of yet another nightmare, these words, these truths, it was still too soon.

Isabella continued. 'I've seen the beer cans in the kitchen. That's not the way. We need to face the truth together, otherwise we can never go forward.'

Sophia sat there, still as tears rolled down her eyes. She listened, taking in the words that were being spoken by her mum. It all made sense. Isabella was right, it was time, but she didn't want her to be right. She closed her eyes, hoping it would all have gone away once she'd opened them, but when she did, everything was the same. Isabella was there, speaking, and Oliver was there staring at the wall, listening.

'This is no way to live,' Isabella said quietly, and so calmly. 'Trust me, I know.' Tears rolled down her eyes as she looked down, ashamed of showing her sadness, but only for a few seconds. She picked herself up, and sat up onto the sofa. She wasn't there for herself.

'The lorry. I need to know, they said something, someone tampering with, or hiring, I don't know, I need to know the truth. Did…' She didn't finish. She looked down, ashamed at the accusation she was about to make.

'Everywhere I go and everything I see reminds me of how things were, when we were happy. How can I let that go? There was so much love.' The sound of sobbing and heartbreak filled the room. Isabella had finally broken through and received words in exchange for hers.

'I know. I'm sorry I should never have…' her voice softened as she spoke, lovingly. 'Nobody is asking you to forget anything. It does take time but it's been nine months and you've kept yourself locked away. You know what you have to do. You can't keep fighting and torturing yourself like this. You have to accept it and let go. I know it's harsh and I'm sorry. It hurts me too, every day, every single day, but it's time to move on.'

Tears rolled down Isabella's face. Sophia hurt even more seeing her mum cry that way. Isabella had cried enough in her lifetime, she'd experienced and seen so much nastiness but still came out on the other side as a beautiful, kind, sweet human being.

Sophia got up and walked to the smaller sofa. She sat on the armrest close to her mum as she cried. She'd felt the pain from listening to the sound of her mother's cries before, and now she was feeling it all over again.

'I'm sorry,' Isabella apologised. 'It's something we can never get over really.' Isabella continued. 'But moving on is something else. Let's take that step together. Come with me, we can go together. I know you haven't been in a long time. Please come with me.'

'I'm sorry too,' Sophia whispered. She kissed her mum on the cheek before standing up. She knew what she had to do.

'Fear ends up causing the most amount of hurt and regret later on in life,' Sophia whispered the words that Oliver had once said to her. It was time. She had to put her mum out of her misery. She had to face her final fear and let go and move on. She didn't wait for Isabella.

Sophia looked around the living room, at her mum, at Oliver, at their selection of DVDs on the shelf, at the pile of papers from Oliver's book that had been sitting on the coffee table. She looked around at the empty bowl of fruit on the table, at the sofa where they'd cosy up and watch films together. She looked at the fireplace, the photos of herself and Oliver on the mantel piece, the ornaments all of the little things that represented their lives together. She looked around and took a deep breath before leaving the room, walking out into the hallway, leaving the house and not looking back. Sophia ran.

She ran down the steps, down the street, past the school, and the blocks of houses. It was dark and the rain was falling hard. Shadows and reflections filled the street as Sophia continued to run, past the church and into the park. She was not afraid.

Sophia knew what she had to do. She ran, as the rain cleansed her body and washed away her tears. She ran.

CHAPTER **THIRTEEN**

The thunder and showers had stopped, and the thick and heavy clouds had moved on to the next town, taking with them the spell of darkness that it carried.

The park was silent and the air was cold but the sun still shone behind the newly formed silver clouds. Yet Sophia was still being followed by the darkness as the shadows from the trees became thicker, taller and blacker than usual as they trailed beside her as she ran.

Sophia ran, through the woodland area, past the hilly slope, the children's play area, and the pond with the fountain. She ran past Lilly's which had closed for the day, as she ran back around, ready to go in for another lap.

'We need to face the truth, otherwise we can never go forward,' she heard her mum's words continuously as they replayed over and over in her ears. 'We can never go forward.'

Sophia was desperate for the pain to stop, for herself, for her mum, and for Oliver. She ran, past the woodland area of the tall trees, past the long grass and bushy hedges, past the children's playground and down a hilly slope. She needed to accept the impacts of her choices, she needed to face the truth and let go, so that everyone she loved could move on.

Sophia felt a burning sensation across her face as the cold air slapped against the warmth of her cheeks. She ran, in and out of the shadows, into the darkness, and back into the light, whilst being beaten and tortured by the icy cold air. She ran, all the way around the park until she reached the beginning, back to the entrance.

Sophia stopped a few meters away from the bench and stared from the distance. A figure was sitting there. He sat forward with his head in his hands. He wore navy blue jeans with light brown trainers, a dark brown leather jacket that had been zipped all the way up with a black and grey striped scarf stuffed inside it. His hair was a mess. This wasn't the man with the blurred face. She knew this figure well.

She walked towards the bench, towards Oliver, slowly, unsure of her next move. She wanted to put her arms around him and tell him it would all be okay but she didn't know herself if it would be.

'It will all be okay in the end, if it's not okay, it's not the end,' she whispered to herself the words that Oliver used to say to her. 'It's not the end if it's not

okay,' she continued with each step. 'It will be okay.'
But she knew it wouldn't ever be okay.

The cold air slapped against her face as she walked
through what seemed like needles as they pricked at
her cheeks. The air remained still and silent as the
sunlight peered down on her, pretending to give her
the warmth that she needed. She wasn't going to let it
deceive her. There was a lot more to it than what it
seemed. She wrapped herself up, tightly as she clung
on to her jacket, refusing to accept the sun's false
heat. She continued to walk towards the bench, ready
to face her truth.

There was no breeze, no movement of the clouds
in the sky or the branches from the trees, and not
even one bird in sight. For that moment, it seemed
Sophia and Oliver had been the only people in the
park. But she knew better.

Sophia continued to walk, slowing down further
the closer she got. She approached the bench and
hesitated as she faced the decision to stay standing, or
sit beside Oliver. She walked to the right of him
before moving back around to his left, confused and
unsure of what she was doing. She waited for the
voices inside her head to instruct her, but they refused
to help. She had ignored them for long enough.

Sophia sat beside him leaving enough space
between them. She didn't need the voices.

The scent of Oliver's aftershave struck her
instantly, making her feel relaxed as it lifted
something positive inside her. She felt a sense of

happiness rise from her body, making her feel light as the scent wrapped around her, hugging her tightly.

She leaned back into the bench, taking a deep breath, awakening her senses as she inhaled Oliver's aftershave. Her body filled with passion as she felt her heart beating, kindly, gently, pumping the love and happiness around her body. For the first time in a long time, Sophia felt alive. The sun beamed onto her face as she looked up, blinding herself from seeing anything other than white light.

Oliver didn't move. He sat forward with his head still down into his hands feeling hopeless. Sophia looked away from the sun and closed her eyes, slowly opening and closing them trying to bring back her vision. The clouds had disappeared.

Ahead of her, in the distance, the figure of a man caught her attention. They weren't alone. The figure stood in the shadows of the trees, leaning against it as though waiting for the right moment to move in.

Sophia closed her eyes again, and opened them, re-adjusting her sight to confirm what she was seeing was real. The man with the blurred face was there. She stared back at him, feeling nothing.

Something inside her had placed a wedge between herself and her fears. It was the same something that had once blocked out anything bad from her mind, and the same something that left her living in a deluded and false life of denial as she went on pretending like everything was perfect in the world of Sophia.

She continued to stare at the figure in the distance as he glared back at her. She didn't react. Instead, her body became limp as she let her muscles fall free, relaxing into the bench. She wasn't going to be afraid anymore. She stayed calm as she sat beside Oliver, trying to feel the power of the strength and positivity he once had inside him, but it no longer existed. His body, pathetic and weak, released waves of fault and negativity as he sat there with his head in his hands. She looked up at the sky again, blocking out having seen this figure watching her, blocking out Oliver's weakness, and the anxiousness that was arising inside of her. She watched as the clouds sat peacefully, perfectly still as though time had stopped. But as Oliver had once told her, 'time waits for no-one.'

The sun looked tired and ready to sleep, despite the beauty of colour that it spread across the sky, golden and deep, like the desert sands, blended with rich hues of red and orange. It was just as beautiful and picturesque as the times when Sophia and Oliver would lay together and watch the sunset. They'd lay there and watch the magical show in the sky as it transformed from one colour to the next, before fading into darkness in a matter of moments. The sky had a split personality of its own.

'Time waits for no-one.' She looked up, and smiled. It had been a long time since she sat with Oliver to see the sunset, even if his head was buried into his hands, they were there in the park. They were there and they were together.

'Happy anniversary,' Sophia whispered in attempt to fill the silence but Oliver ignored her as he had done earlier that morning. His head stayed submerged inside his hands. He didn't react.

She closed her eyes, still facing the sky, looking to God for support and assurance, becoming desperate to block out the voices that were beginning to takeover inside her head. She took a deep breath, ready to speak.

'I went to the church today,' her voice trembled. It was time to accept the truth. 'We should have gone together Ol, it was only meant to be us going together. But I did it. And I faced my fear and I went in on my own and I prayed. I prayed for you Ol.'

Oliver sat with his head still placed into his hands. The park was still empty with no sign of life other than Sophia, Oliver, and the figure in the distance. He stood there against the tree, still far away, but this time a little closer than he had been before.

Sophia's body began to feel weaker and frail as the wedge began to loosen from her mind. The sharpness of the cold air continued to bite at her skin and her face started to become even more dull and pale with every breath she took. She sat there looking up at the sky, knowing she was being watched, knowing he was waiting. Anxiety took over as she came to realise she was no longer running away. This was new and she wasn't used to it. Her heart began to beat faster, her hands sticky with cold sweat. Her shoulders lifted and tightened. The voices inside her head began to talk, loud and all at once, telling her to get up, telling her to run. The wedge had gone. She began to panic, confused as she looked around, at the trees, the sky, the man.

The sound of Oliver sniffling drowned out the voices. Sophia turned to look at him. His head was still down, leaning into his hands. He needed her. Everything around her disappeared as she looked at him, crying silently to himself. He needed her, and almost instantly, nothing else mattered.

Sophia lifted her arm towards Oliver and began to run her fingers gently across the back of his head. She moved her hand towards the top of his head, rubbing his scalp softly, and running her fingers along his long, brown hair. Oliver had always found it relaxing.

'I asked God,' Sophia's voice was soothing and calm. She continued to glide her fingers through Oliver's hair, as she spoke to him, softly. 'I asked God to give me a sign because I don't see it,' she moved closer to Oliver. 'I'm lost. I feel empty, like you've walked away from me. You walked away from me and my mums right, I need to let go, for both of our sakes but I can't.' She began to cry, moving her arm away from Oliver. She leaned forward and placed her head in her hands, covering her eyes, hiding her tears.

The atmosphere around them became colder and a gust of air moved past them. It was a sign. Sophia knew she was going to be face to face with the figure in the distance, soon. But she wasn't ready.

'This is my fault, the reason why we're sitting here

like this, it's all because of my own mistakes and no matter what I do, I won't ever be able to undo it.'

A shadow invaded the space in front of her, blocking out the light from the sun. Fear ran through Sophia's body like electricity, and panic surrounded her. She hadn't said goodbye. She wasn't ready yet, to face her fears, to finally come face to face with this figure. She was desperate to stop Oliver's tears, even if it meant being deluded and accepting all fault. She needed to speak to him. Sophia opened her eyes.

Isabella walked around to stand beside the bench. She didn't sit down, nor did she speak. Sophia closed her eyes and relaxed her shoulders. She still had time.

'I can't come back from what's already happened.' She continued with her eyes closed, tightly, blocking out Isabella's presence. 'Maybe our time together was always meant to be short. I'm holding on to someone who I can't be with, you're already letting me go. That's why you're here aren't you? That's why you did it.' Sophia sobbed with her head placed into her hands, continuing to hide her face and the tears that filled her eyes. Oliver sat there, quietly as he continued to ignore her. 'I'm sorry I couldn't take care of you the way I wanted to,' her speech was muffled but it didn't matter. No-one was listening. She refused to say any more.

Neither Oliver nor Isabella uttered a word. Minutes had passed and the park became silent again as both Sophia and Oliver sat quietly on the bench with their heads down, thinking about how they ended up there. So much had changed so quickly.

'We can never go forward.' She heard Isabella's voice inside her head. She didn't want to be the reason why they were trapped. She knew exactly how it felt, being stuck in a cage for everyone to see.

Sophia took a deep breath and sat up, stretching her spine and wiping the tears from her face. She looked up, eyes strong and focused on the man in the distance. She'd found her strength through her mum's words. It was time to set them free.

'Soulmates will always find a way, just remember that Ol. There are some things in life we just can't control, but you already know that.' She sat there, gazing at the man in the distance, peacefully. 'And there are some things you can. You know that too. Happiness. Don't forget that.' Sophia was content with her fate. She smiled. Sophia was ready.

Gold, red and orange leaves began to fall from the sky. It was winter and the trees no longer bore any leaves, yet the colours of the autumn began to fill the space over her. Sophia looked up, confused and amazed as these colourful leaves fell gently from above her. They fell from way beyond the bare trees, and beyond the clouds in the sky. She smiled at the magic within the atmosphere that now surrounded her. She loved the magnificent colours of nature. As the leaves landed on the ground, they formed a magical pathway of gold, red and orange from the bench all the way to the figure in the distance. He was now moving closer. She looked up at the sun as it moved slowly, preparing to set. Tears began to roll down her cheeks as she realised this would be the last sunset she'd see with Oliver beside her. She closed her eyes, tightly, recalling some of the most cherished and happiest moments during their seventeen years together.

She thought back to the first time they met, when Lucy introduced the two back in school, and his reaction when he caught her reading his notes. She smiled as she saw the beauty in his eyes as he gave her the mosaic mirror, and the embarrassed look on his face when she'd seen his 'to do' list timeline. She pictured him and his mismatched sense of fashion, and saw the cheeky grin on his face and the light in his eyes each time he ate watermelon. She felt their first kiss, the sensation of being loved and the warmth she felt inside when he gave her the heart stone. She heard his gentle voice as he sang *Is This Love?* and the look in his eyes as he sang, from his soul to hers. She saw them dancing together in the spare room, laughing and giggling together, playing around and teasing each other. She thought of the night when they were stuck in the car in Scotland and the love she felt inside her as she watched him sleep peacefully beside her. She thought of the riddles and quizzes they did together, laying there on the sofa, listening to music and watching YouTube videos on their phones. She went back to the moment she started to believe in soulmates after feeling a strong wave of electricity pass through his hand and into hers as they lay together whilst watching a film. She felt the flutter of her heart and the certainty of their love as they exchanged rings. She saw the proud look on his face when she drove the car for the first time without panicking, and when she eventually did her bungee jump. She had flashbacks of every moment, every anniversary, every birthday and everything good. She continued to reminisce over the years until her smile began to fall as the happy memories turned into sad. She saw Oliver's eyes, glazed with tears as she looked at him in the hospital, holding her hand and sitting beside her. She saw him, heart-broken and distant as his face became thin, and body more frail. She watched as he began to slow down and deteriorate as days went by. Tears rolled down her face as she saw him hide back his tears as he looked down at the coffin.

'It's time Oliver.' Isabella placed her hand on his shoulder.

'She's right Soph,' Oliver whispered. 'I need to say goodbye,' he wiped the corner of his eye. 'I love you,' he whispered. 'I set you free.'

'I love you so much more,' Sophia's eyes remained closed, she couldn't watch him leave. Isabella became numb.

Silence conquered the park. The sun had set, like a deflated balloon, leaving behind a dull orange haze as it began to disappear in the horizon. The park was now scattered with spots of artificial dim lighting from the little lampposts in the distance. Sophia opened her eyes. The colourful path became illuminated as it came to life with an aura of bright blue light around it.

Isabella and Oliver had gone.

Sophia sat on the bench, feeling empty and cold. Oliver had gone. There was nothing else to it, it was time. She put her hands together and turned her head down towards the foot of the bench as something glistened in the corner of her eye. Beside her sat a beautiful heart stone.

Sophia's soul filled with love, electricity and a mix of happy feelings that she hadn't felt in a long time. She reached for the heart stone and ran her fingers along one side before turning it over and running her fingers along the other side. She held it tight, towards her chest and closed her eyes. She took a deep breath as she held the heart close to hers.

'I love you Oliver Cane. In this life time, in the life time before, and in every life time to come.' She opened her eyes and looked towards the figure.

Sophia was ready.

CHAPTER **FOURTEEN**

Isabella had taken a taxi home, silently, not having said a word, as if she'd heard nothing. But the words replayed over and over inside her head, 'I set you free.' She sat in the back of the taxi, in shock, in horror, numb, praying it wasn't *that*.

Oliver sat on the sofa, alone. He was still in his jacket and trainers as he sat there in the dark, in the company of all of the obscured shadows that had been created by the dim light from the lamppost outside. He sat there, still fixated on the crack in the wall, which within the shadows, seemed like it was just a blur. But he'd spent enough time staring at it, that it had become engrained into his vision. He was able to see it clearly, even when he was asleep.

He re-examined each part of the crack, like reading a map after taking a wrong turn, trying to figure out where he was, where he'd gone wrong. He stared at it as an attempt to block out the thoughts that were running through his mind. He sat there, still and stiff, like a robot, refusing to cry, refusing to break down, and refusing to be the scared little boy he once used to be.

He didn't blink.

***

March 8 2017. It was a Friday afternoon and Oliver had just come back from the hospital. He was exhausted and still in shock as he stood there in the middle of the living room, staring at the wall, spellbound and in a trance of numbness. His eyes were small, puffy and red and his face was sweaty and soaked in tears, his hair was rough and uncombed, and he hadn't shaved in days.

He stood and looked around him, at the room and everything inside it. He was surrounded by Sophia's warmth. The photos on the mantle of the fireplace, the colours of the ornaments and furnishings, the placing of the little cushions that sat on the sofa, the DVD collection on the shelf, everything around him was Sophia. He stood there, taking it all in, surrounded by her soul.

His mobile phone began to vibrate in the pocket of his jeans, buzzing through his ears and distracting him, creating a distance between himself and Sophia.

He stood still, with his eyes focused on the mantle of the fireplace, trying to ignore the buzzing from his pocket. He was drawn to a photo that sat there, looking back at him. Sophia's face sparkled ahead of him, smiling at him. Her arms were wrapped around him, squeezing him tightly. Both of their eyes beamed with happiness as they sat there, posing for the camera.

Oliver's phone continued to buzz from his pocket. He walked over to the photo frame, continuing to ignore the call until it eventually stopped vibrating.

He picked up the frame and ran his fingers along Sophia's face as he examined the beauty of the two of them together. He could feel her holding him with all of the love inside her as she pressed her face against his, their eyes glistening, and smiles shining. He held the frame to his chest and turned to move towards the sofa.

The buzzing from his pocket started again. Oliver placed the photo frame onto the coffee table and took a seat on the sofa opposite. His eyes glazed over with tears as he stared into Sophia's eyes. His phone continued to buzz.

He stared at Sophia's photo long and hard, gazing into her eyes. The buzzing continued. He closed his eyes tightly, trying to feel Sophia with him, but the buzzing filled his ears, becoming louder and louder the more he tried to avoid it. Oliver stood up and took out his phone from his pocket, throwing it hard against the wall in front of him. The phone stopped buzzing instantly as it shattered against the wall, leaving a little crack.

He sat back onto the sofa, and cried as he stared into Sophia's eyes.

***

Oliver stayed on the sofa for at least five minutes glaring at the crack in the wall, recalling the night his life was taken away from him over and over again. He stood and walked over to the mantle of the fireplace, picking up the same photo of himself and Sophia, recreating the moment from nine months ago all over again as he placed it on the coffee table and sat back down on the sofa opposite.

He closed his eyes thinking back to the days before that night, wishing things had gone differently.

***

It was March 3 2017. The sunlight came beaming into the bedroom, bouncing off the walls and spreading warmth into the air, embracing both Sophia and Oliver. The sound of the birds, chirping and singing on the rooftop and along the branches of the tree opposite the house, chimed through the window. The smell of freshly cut grass mixed with homemade bread filled the house.

Sophia and Oliver had just come upstairs to carry out all of the last minute preparations for their trip to Lake Como. They were going away for Sophia's thirty-fifth birthday, celebrating for the first time since her dads passing. Oliver had wanted to make it perfect for her and had organised a two week holiday away. He'd been to Lake Como before, and wanted to experience the outstanding views with Sophia.

'I'll have a quick shower and then get on this.' Oliver was sweaty from having mown the lawn in their back garden.

They had a day until they were due to fly and were yet to do their final checks, making sure they'd packed all the essentials for their break.

'Okay. Did you pack the camera?' Sophia asked as she checked through her suitcase.

'Yep, I put it in your hand luggage. I think the charger needs to go in though.' Oliver moved to the cupboard to find the camera charger. 'You've got the locks right?' he asked whilst rummaging through a range of laptop and phone chargers.

'Oh! I'll send mum a message now and ask her to get them out.' Sophia picked up her phone and began to search for Isabella's number. She'd given the locks to their suitcases to Isabella to use when she went away to Spain for a few days over Christmas and had forgotten to pick them up.

'Want me to get them?' Oliver asked as he struggled to untangle the lead of the camera charger from the rest of them.

'It's okay. I'll be back by the time you're out the shower. I haven't seen mum for about three days anyway so I'll go,' she said as she looked down at her phone texting Isabella. 'It's a nice day for a walk.'

Sophia smiled and looked up at Oliver.

'Wouldn't it be quicker if you drove?' As well as the trip to Lake Como, Oliver had bought Sophia a car of her own so she could be more independent and free to go wherever she wanted, whenever she wanted, without needing to wait for him to be home. It was an early birthday present that he gave to Sophia earlier that day over breakfast.

'Or I could just walk Ol, it's a nice day outside,' she repeated.

'The sun is shining. Let's go together, later on,' he finally managed to untangle all of the leads from the camera charger. He smiled as he walked over to Sophia handing her the charger to pack in her suitcase, knowing she'd want to get the packing done sooner rather than later.

'Hmmm. I need to stick the washing on, finish packing, wash my hair. So much to do. It'll be easier if I just go now.' She looked at Oliver. 'I'll drive.' She couldn't disagree with him twice. 'I'll be back by the time you're out the shower and we can finish off packing.' She continued to text Isabella. 'I'll take some of our homemade bread for her too, she'd like that.'

***

A tear ran down Oliver's face as he sat there alone on his living room sofa, retracing his thoughts back to the moment that changed his life. He sat there, thinking about all the 'what if's,' coming up with different scenarios, and wishing things had gone differently.

The room was still as cold as it was when he walked in, if not more. He sat there, trying to put into practice what he'd spent most of his life trying to preach. He sat there, trying to recognise his feelings, trying to understand his emotions, to accept the truth and just carry on. The phone began to ring but Oliver didn't move. He let it go to the answering machine.

'Hi, sorry we're not here to take your call right now…' He listened to the sound of Sophia's voice on the answering machine as he sunk right back into the sofa and closed his eyes. He took a deep breath, leaving his eyes closed tightly as he held back the tears he'd spent months keeping in.

'But please leave a message after the beep and we'll get back to you when we can,' his voice followed.

There was no sound other than rustling coming from the machine. Someone was on the other end of the phone but no-one spoke. Oliver sat still, waiting for them to leave him alone. They hung up.

***

Sophia ran down the stairs, grabbing the keys to her new car from the key rack on the wall before running out the door and down the steps. Isabella's home was only a five minute drive away.

She stepped into her new car, adjusting her seat and side mirrors before moving off for the first time, feeling confident and happy. Oliver stood and watched from the window of their bedroom, taking his towel that had been hanging from the handle of the exercise bike. He watched as a dark cloud glazed over his marble-like eyes. A smile spread across his face. He was proud of her, proud of himself.

***

Oliver was interrupted by the sound of the phone ringing as it filled the room again. He took a deep breath, annoyed at not being able to think in peace.

'Hi, sorry we're not here to take your call right now…' He listened to the sound of Sophia's voice on the answering machine again.

'But please leave a message after the beep and we'll get back to you when we can,' his voice followed.

This time, the cries of a baby filled the room.

'Oli, seriously. You need to meet her! Why aren't you here already?' Tristan was speaking loudly trying to over-power the sound of his daughter's cries. 'Sophia is waiting for you.' He hung up.

Oliver's face instantly relaxed. His eyes were still closed but he was now in deep thought. The tightness in his face and body moved away from him as a gracious feeling overcame him. His face became soft and peaceful and his body relaxed further into the sofa. Hearing Sophia's name for the first time in so long made him feel light. The weight lifted from inside his body. Finally, someone spoke of her name.

'Sophia,' he whispered to himself as a hint of a smile crossed his face. He sat there, with his eyes closed, smiling to himself, as he watched her smiling back at him.

At least an hour had passed and Oliver was still sitting on the sofa, laying back with his eyes closed. He was calm, relaxed. He opened his eyes and sat forward.

'I set you free Soph. I hope you're happier.' He stood from the sofa and smiled again. He walked up the stairs and into the spare room towards the shelving unit before picking out a pen and a little book. He began to write.

December 16th 2017

Today is a good day Soph. I miss you, so much. I know I said this was all meant to be positive, I haven't really been sticking by it have I? I will. I'm sorry. I know I can talk to you about all of the positives, and there will be many. I've been given a second chance Soph, again. I'm going to see our little niece, one step at a time. I'm going to see Sophia, I bet she's a beauty. Do you remember when you said you'll be the favourite? You were right. I'll tell her all about you. I promise. Be free now.

Oliver closed his journal and ran his fingers over the lion before placing it back on the shelf. He walked out of the room and into the bathroom. He splashed his face with cold water and patted it dry with a towel, before walking into the bedroom.

He took out his blue jeans and a grey jumper from his wardrobe. The jumper still had tags on it. It was a random gift from Sophia earlier that year but he never had the chance to wear it. Oliver ripped off the tags and changed out of his joggers and sweatshirt and into the jumper and jeans as he looked at himself in the mirror. His marble-like eyes glistened as he smiled.

He was going to see Sophia.

CHAPTER FIFTEEN

The air was still. The gold, red, and orange carpet of leaves was still illuminated with a bright blue aura as though they had been floating on a magical river. The leaves below Sophia's feet sparkled, and the tranquil sounds of water flowing peacefully along the newly formed pathway soothed her.

Sophia looked around. The rest of the park was filled with dark shadows. The same shadows that had been haunting her in her nightmares, and the same shadows that she had been running from in her reality. She was no longer afraid. No longer afraid of the voices inside her head, no longer afraid of being alone, and no longer afraid of what was really happening. She was at peace.

She rested her body, realising she had escaped. She had escaped from her fear and paranoia, from her pain, her torture and all the truths and lies that she buried within her. She had escaped from the voices inside her head, and everything that made her delusional, everything that she had been ignoring and running away from.

She felt awakened, as if a flame had been ignited inside her, giving her the strength and power to be the lion that she was meant to be. No-one was going to hold her back. Not this time. The fire burned inside her, warming her body, taking her away from the coldness and shedding light into the place that had been filled with darkness. She felt human again. Free. Imaginary wings spread out from her sides as she pictured all of the places that she could go and all of the things that she could do. She was free.

She looked down at the heart stone she was holding in her hands and closed her eyes. She smiled as she saw Oliver's dark, marble eyes staring into hers. It was time to let go. Sophia was at peace.

The sound of rustling in the distance awakened her from her thoughts. She opened her eyes to see the figure move towards her in the shadows. She watched as the man with the blurred face moved closer, slowly, with his face down, eyes on her. It was time to accept the final truth, and find her way out.

Sophia closed her eyes again, holding on to the heart stone, giving this figure the time he needed to approach her. She sat up straight on the bench, eyes still closed. A cold breeze began to fill the air around her and she felt a sudden chill down her spine and into her body. He was there. She opened her eyes.

219

The man stood in front of her, in his muddy blue jeans and his unzipped, dark brown bomber jacket over a navy blue hoodie, his face was down but his eyes were on her. His body stood as he arched over her as she sat, looking up at him from the bench. His face was no longer blurred. She recognised him, she always recognised him.

She wiped a tear from her eye. 'Let's go,' she whispered. But the man moved to sit beside her. She still had time. She didn't flinch. They sat silently together as Sophia closed her eyes. The fire continued to burn inside her, warming her soul.

***

The sun was shining brightly and Sophia was excited for their trip to Lake Como.

'Love you mum!' she yelled as she ran from the front door of her mum's house, inches away from bumping into an old man walking his dog.

'Morning,' he said cheerfully, even though it was the afternoon. She smiled back, apologising at the same time as she got into her car.

She waved to Isabella through the window, blowing her a kiss before she turned on the engine. Ed Sheeran's *Shape of You* was playing through the car speakers. Sophia turned up the volume before setting off down the road.

For the first time, she felt confident driving despite it being her first time in her new car. She drove happily singing along to *Shape of You*. They were going to Lake Como in less than twenty four hours. Life was good.

She slowed down as she came to a zebra crossing, stopping to let a lady pass. The lady walked along slowly, with an empty pushchair. A little girl followed behind as she stared at Sophia, smiling. Sophia smiled back as she waited for them to cross over before she moved forward, turning onto the main road. Ed Sheeran continued to sing in the background as Sophia joined in with a duet. A sudden flicker of light caught her eye in her side mirror, as her rear view mirror filled with the flashing lights of an ambulance. It was right behind her, flashing at her, telling her to move. Her palms became sweaty as she panicked, slowing down nervously as she moved to the side letting it pass before moving back out. She panicked, wondering how long the ambulance was behind her, feeling guilty for being a bad driver. She looked to the buttons and dials on the dashboard to turn down the volume. A loud sound of a horn echoed through her ears and horror filled her eyes as she looked into her rear view mirror. A large lorry had been tailing the ambulance, coming in at full speed towards the back of her car. She panicked and tried to swerve away but it was too late. The lorry slammed into the back of her car so hard that it sent her fragile body flying into the steering wheel, crushing her chest instantly. The impact sent the car swerving 360 degrees to the right and into the lane opposite within seconds as another car smashed into her side door, crushing her legs on impact.

Shattered glass flew into her face and her eyes were filled with blood. She was deafened by the sound of horns and sirens that filled her ears, while the smell of burnt rubber scorched her nostrils. She sat in the car with her head slumped forward, leaning to one side with only the seatbelt holding her up. She fell into unconsciousness.

Two hours had passed and Sophia was awoken by the sound of drilling as firefighters attempted to cut through the doors and seats, trying to get her out. Her ears were ringing and her head was thumping, vision blurred. She was confused and unable to move. She closed her eyes and fell in and out of consciousness.

For days she lay in hospital, unable to move or speak. She watched as Oliver, Isabella, Tristan and Lucy stood beside her bed, each of them praying, talking to her, stroking her head and holding her hands. She listened as they spoke to her, to each other, reminiscing about their days in school and during sixth form. She watched as their eyes carried sadness and fear as they began to lose hope as each day went by. She watched as they put on brave faces as they told her stories of what they all still had planned to do together, lying to her with love, about going home, and going away to Lake Como. She watched as they spoke to her with positivity, giving her hope, although they'd lost theirs. And she watched as they tried to make her comfortable, because they knew they could do no more.

***

'I should never have got into the car,' she whispered.

The man stood and began to lead the way, walking along the carpet of leaves. He stopped a meter away, realising Sophia wasn't following behind. He stood and stared off into the distance as he waited patiently.

The moon shone bright. It was large and low like a big torch, spilling it's light across the sky, bathing the park with silver, further illuminating the magical carpet of leaves. The sky was freckled with glittered stars as they sparkled from the heavens above.

Sophia stood and looked ahead at the silhouette of the man in front of her who was now holding out his arm for her to take hold of. She turned to the bench and ran her fingers along a small engraved plaque that had been drilled into it. She smiled, as she accepted her fate as she placed the heart stone back where Oliver had left it. It wasn't hers to keep.

'It's time to let go,' she whispered as she looked towards the magical path. She walked towards the man.

'Let's go princess,' he took her hand as they walked along the path and into the light.

The park remained silent as the moonlight glistened against the small plaque on the bench.

In loving memory of Sophia Cane, 1982 – 2017.

CHAPTER **SIXTEEN**

Living every day as if it were your last, by Oliver Cane

Life works in strange ways. One minute you're sitting there, happy and content, with friends and family around you. You've got it all going for you. A cosy and comfortable home, one where you can watch the sunset every day out of your window, a place of peace and tranquillity in your house and within your soul, a place to fulfil your dreams with your partner beside you, supporting you as they fulfill theirs. You had that spark, poured gasoline over it to make it stronger, but it explodes. Vanishes. Gone. It's all gone, taken away, removed. Because you were greedy. Greedy for her. And now you're a monster who would do anything to survive. Rationality doesn't exist and the world is either black or white.

Giving up is, and has always been the easier option, but never always the right one. In times of darkness, in times of hatred and evil, where our own deepest, darkest secrets of time eat at us every single day, it is important to find the strength to overcome it, to forgive yourself and those around you, and focus on what's actually important - life.

People come and people go. Sometimes out of choice – yours or theirs, and sometimes there is no choice. But for as long as you are on this planet, life does go on. I've always believed that time waits for no-one. Time never stops, even when you do, so you just have to carry on.

Everyone gets chances and opportunities, no matter how big or small. What do you want in life? What have you always wanted out of life? What are you doing to get it?

Every dream begins with a dreamer. As long as your heart is beating, you will have time to make yours a reality. Kings will dream, but only you can make yours come true. Let me teach you how.

I'm Oliver Cane, and this is my ~~story~~ confession.

ACKNOWLEDGEMENTS

Many people helped me over the time it took me to write this book, knowingly or not. A huge thank you to my mum and dad, Prabha and Narendra Manani, my sister, Nisha Patel, and my niece, Shreya Patel, who remained patient with me during the times I would lock myself away, focusing on writing.

An extra thank you goes to Shreya for having that patience and understanding at a young age, and for sharing an interest in the storyline and the characters in this novel throughout my time writing it. Thank you for the motivation my sweet baby.

My gratitude goes to my brother in law, Minesh Patel, my aunty, Madhu Manani, and my two cousins, Sonal Manani and Pria Carr, for taking the time to read the initial draft. They provided me with genuine feedback and advice on how to make this novel stronger, and their enthusiasm made me feel that much more positive.

A double thank you goes to Pria who was eight months pregnant whilst proofing, so thank you baby Arin James Carr for letting mummy read what she could peacefully. Welcome to the world.

To my cousin, Mayuri Sachin Tailor, thank you for the encouragement, for sharing the same level of excitement with me, and for constantly asking, 'how's the book coming along?' even though you got the same answer back each time – 'still going,' followed by either a sigh or way too much energy from my end, thanks for reciprocating the energy back.

Thank you to my best friends who are also my family, Manpreet Sandhu, Amarpreet Kaur Sohal, and Jagpal Kaur Johal for the constant positivity and support – talking to you girls about the book made it all feel so real.

I'm also thankful to attitude and psychological development coach, Gavin Drake at Mindspan, who opened my eyes to where I needed to invest my time and energy to get what I truly wanted from life. Thank you, and thank you to my old boss, James Blower, for introducing the sessions to the team in the first place. This is where it all began.

My greatest debt goes to a previous friend who believed in the concept of *The Colours of Denial* from the beginning, and continuously encouraged and inspired me to take that first step. Sinth, if it wasn't for you, this may have become just another book I started and given up on. Thank you.

And finally, thank you to every single person who has genuinely supported me with their kind words and excitement, be it via phone, in person, or through social media, it truly has motivated me to keep going. Because of your ongoing support, positivity and belief that I could do this, I was able to. It means everything – thank you all. Sending high-fives, hearts and smiley face emoji's to you all. Yay! We did it.

Find Arti on Instagram @Author_Arti_Manani
#TheColoursOfDenial

Printed in Great Britain
by Amazon

36580392R00142